五|集|纪|录|片

山西省人民政府新闻办公室　编

北岳文艺出版社 ·太原·　　NEWSTAR PRESS 新星出版社 ·北京·

图书在版编目（CIP）数据

寻踪晋商 / 山西省人民政府新闻办公室编 . -- 太原：北岳文艺出版社；北京：新星出版社，2024.8.
ISBN 978-7-5378-6904-1

Ⅰ. I25

中国国家版本馆 CIP 数据核字第 2024KL3415 号

寻踪晋商
XUNZONG JINSHANG

山西省人民政府新闻办公室 / 编

//

出品人
郭文礼
马汝军

选题策划
郭文礼
邹懿男

责任编辑
武慧敏
林 琳

封面设计
薛 菲

内文设计
王利锋

印装监制
郭 勇

出版发行：山西出版传媒集团·北岳文艺出版社
地址：山西省太原市并州南路 57 号　　邮编：030012
电话：0351-5628696（发行部）0351-5628688（总编室）
传真：0351-5628680
经销商：新华书店
印刷装订：山西新华印业有限公司

开本：787 mm × 1092 mm　　1/16
字数：186 千
印张：16.25
插页：6
版次：2024 年 8 月第 1 版
印次：2024 年 8 月山西第 1 次印刷
书号：ISBN 978-7-5378-6904-1
定价：98.00 元

本书版权为本社独家所有，未经本社同意不得转载、摘编或复制

万里茶道总图

《万里茶道总图》 张喜琴 刘建生 绘　General Map of Ten Thousand Miles of Tea Ceremony, by Zhang Xiqin and Liu Jiansheng

纪录片《寻踪晋商》职员表

总 策 划：张吉福

策　　划：宋　伟　张　羽　骞　进　万　勇　杨建军

总 监 制：刘英魁

监　　制：胡　芸　陈　霞

总 撰 稿：陈　霞　焦中栋

顾　　问：张正明　杜学文　高春平　刘建生　靳　斌

学术专家：王茹芹　周建波　魏明孔　赵　磊　兰日旭
　　　　　王书华　石　涛　刘成虎　张宪平　乔　南
　　　　　张维东

导 演 组：郭　松　姚丽菊　阴文丽　王　鑫　余亚茹

节目统筹：靳　然　蔡福涛

摄 像 组：张志中　韩　鹏　樊茂盛　籍少华　逯　鹏
　　　　　牛晓峰　张　卓　李昊洋　高东辉　闫志平
　　　　　马旭峰　张志峰　陈炜坚

剪 辑 组：高幸幸　李佳阳　李彦玲　张　强

包 装 组：周诘郲　吉　涛　祁　江　王恺玥　王晓飞　胡　琳
　　　　　王悦泽　胡崇阳　刘　崟　谢春娇　赵艳琰

虚拟场景制作组：
　　　　　周志成　李　冰　吴　杰　宋巍巍　阎世文　朱志杰
　　　　　简莹蓉　陈　巍　李雅玲　李京航　胡梦奇　石　科

情景再现摄制组：
　　　　　赵华琳　周　峰　田延星　支建庆　田育红　刘月春
　　　　　杨鹏飞　史　攀　党慧萍　张晓云　郭建波　武小虎

作曲/声音制作：
　　　　　凌　青　刘　颖　黄钧业　张　恒　冯明枭　孙　健
　　　　　闫　沛　张旭东　赵　宇　李富康　史晗相

解　　说：杨　晨

责任编辑：杨艳菲　申　倩

导演助理：郭　嘉　李梦菲　贾渊渊　田诗桐　张　腾　李可渲
　　　　　李未晚　赵星荷　张思捷　王晨阳　李嘉乐

前 言

习近平总书记视察山西时指出:"山西自古就有重商文化传统,形成了诚实守信、开拓进取、和衷共济、务实经营、经世济民的晋商精神。"在悠悠岁月的长河中,晋商宛如一颗璀璨夺目的明珠,散发着独特而耀眼的光芒。

明清晋商,纵横欧亚九千里,称雄商界五百年。他们以诚实守信的道德支撑、开拓进取的奋斗精神、和衷共济的价值追求、务实经营的商业智慧、经世济民的天下情怀镌刻在历史的记忆中。他们的传奇故事,不仅仅是一部波澜壮阔的商业史诗,更是一部蕴含着深邃智慧、无畏勇气、诚信道义和家国担当的宏大篇章。

为深入挖掘、弘扬、展示晋商的当代价值和世界意义,增强文化自信,开辟新的征程,山西省人民政府新闻办公室和山西广播电视台联合出品了五集纪录片《寻踪晋商》。纪录片一经播出,获得社会各界热烈反响,并译成多种语言向世界推广。为进一步扩大该片传播力影响力,我们策划出版了同名图书《寻踪晋商》。当我们轻轻翻开这部《寻踪晋商》,仿佛悄然打开了一扇通往历史深邃之处的神秘大门,晋商那伟岸而坚毅的身影逐渐清晰地呈现在我们的眼前。

晋商的智慧，犹如璀璨的繁星，令人赞叹不已。他们始终坚定不移地坚守着"以义制利"的崇高原则，一诺千金，童叟无欺。这份对诚信的执着坚守，如同熠熠生辉的灯塔，照亮了他们前行的道路。他们善于推陈出新，敢于冲破传统商业模式的束缚，开创性地构建了许多前所未有的经营策略和金融工具。票号的应运而生，无疑是晋商智慧的璀璨结晶。它宛如一场革新的风暴，彻底改变了商业资金流转的固有方式，为经济的蓬勃发展注入了源源不断的强大动力。与此同时，晋商还高度注重团队的协同合作，通过精心构建严密有序的组织架构和科学完善的管理制度，成功实现了商业运作的规模化和规范化发展，使其商业帝国得以高效运转，日益强大。

然而，晋商的辉煌成就并不仅仅局限于商业领域的累累硕果，更体现在他们深沉厚重的家国情怀之中。当国家深陷危难之际，他们挺身而出，毫不吝啬地慷慨解囊，倾尽全力救国家于危难中；当社会迫切需要援助之时，他们义无反顾，毫不犹豫地伸出援手，以实际行动诠释着"达则兼济天下"的博大胸怀，为后世树立了光辉的典范。

在深入探寻晋商的发展足迹时，我们被他们的传奇经历深深触动，他们从广袤的黄土地出发，心怀炽热的梦想和无尽的希望，毅然决然地踏上了那条充满未知挑战与无限机遇的漫漫征程。一代又一代山西商人在艰苦卓绝中开辟"世纪动脉"万里茶道，首创票号汇兑业务"汇通天下"，创造了"纵横欧亚九千里，称雄商界五百年"的商业辉煌，走出一条商业文明演进的中国式道路。他们所历经的风雨沧桑，所铸就的辉煌成就，都已成为中华民族璀璨商业文明不可或缺的重要组成部分。

希望广大读者朋友们在阅读的过程中，能够与晋商展开一场跨越时空的心灵对话，深入体会其中蕴含的奋斗力量和智慧宝藏。亲身感受那段波澜壮阔的历史征程，尽情领略那份历久弥新、永不褪色的精神魅力！

PREFACE

During his visit to Shanxi, General Secretary Xi Jinping pointed out that "Shanxi has had a tradition of mercantile culture since ancient times, forming the spirit of the Shanxi merchants who are honest and trustworthy, pioneering and enterprising, harmonious and helpful, pragmatic in business, and helpful to the people through the world". In the long history, Shanxi merchants are like a dazzling pearl, emitting a unique and dazzling light.

Shanxi merchants in the Ming and Qing Dynasties, who have travelled across Europe and Asia for nine thousand miles, have dominated the business world for five hundred years. They were supported by moral honesty and trustworthiness, and their pioneering and enterprising spirit of struggle, the pursuit of harmony and communion, the business wisdom of pragmatic management, and the world sentiment of the world's people have been engraved in the memory of history. Their legendary story is not only a magnificent business epic, but also a grand chapter containing profound wisdom, fearless courage, honesty, morality, and national responsibility.

In order to deeply excavate, promote and demonstrate the contemporary value and world significance of Shanxi merchants, enhance cultural confidence and open up a new journey, the Information Office of the People's Government of Shanxi Province and Shanxi Radio and Television Station jointly produced a five-episode documentary film called Tracing Shanxi Merchants. Once aired, the documentary received warm response from all walks of life and was translated into many languages for worldwide dissemination. In order to further expand the influence of the film's dissemination power, we planned and published a book with the same title. When we gently flick through the book Tracing Shanxi Merchants, it is as if we have quietly opened a mysterious door to the depths of history, and the great and resolute figure of Jin merchants is gradually and clearly presented in front of our eyes.

The wisdom of Shanxi merchants is like a bright star, which is admired from one's deep heart. They have always been steadfastly adhering to the noble principle, making profits with righteousness, and have always been true to their word. This persistent adherence to credibility is like a glittering lighthouse and illuminates their way forward. They are good at innovation, dare to break the boundaries of the traditional business model, pioneering the construction of many unprecedented business strategies and financial tools. The birth of the exchange shop is undoubtedly the brilliant creation by intelligent Shanxi merchants. It is like a storm of innovation, completely changing the inherent way of commercial capital flows, and continually injecting the strong power for the vigorous development of the economy. At the same time, Shanxi merchants also pay great attention to teamwork, and successfully achieve the scaled and regulated business operations through the careful construction of a strict and orderly organizational structure and a scientific and perfect management system, so that their business empire can operate efficiently and become more and more powerful.

Furthermore, the brilliant achievements of Shanxi merchants are not limited to the commercial field alone, but are also reflected in their deep patriotism. When the country was in deep crisis, they stepped forward and gave generously without stint, doing their best to save the country from danger. When the society was in urgent need of assistance, they did not hesitate to lend a helping hand, interpreting the broad-mindedness of "to achieve is to help the world at large" with practical actions, and setting up a glorious model for the future generations.

When exploring the development footprints of Shanxi merchants, we were deeply touched by their legendary experience. They set off from the vast Loess Plateau, with burning dreams and endless hopes, and started on a long journey full of unknown challenges and unlimited opportunities without hesitation. Generations of Shanxi merchants struggled to open up the Miles Tea Route, which called the 'The Artery of the Century'. Their original exchange business was world-famous. And their 9,000-mile Eurasian commercial route was an unquestionable human miracle! Shanxi Merchants have worked out a Chinese-style path of the evolution of commercial civilization. The difficulties and hardships they have been through and the brilliant achievements they have forged have become an indispensable and important part of the bright commercial civilization of the Chinese nation.

It is hoped that readers and friends will be able to start a spiritual dialogue with Shanxi merchants across time and space, and deeply appreciate the power of struggle and the treasure of wisdom contained therein during reading this book. Moreover, feeling the magnificent historical journey and enjoying the everlasting and never-fading spiritual charm!

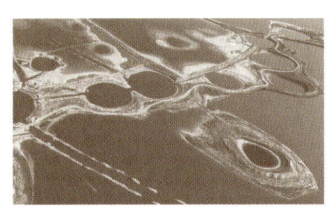

第一章　山西商人的崛起
Part 1　The Rise of Shanxi Merchants

001

第二章　建造辉煌的商业王国
Part 2　The Magnificent Commercial Empire

049

第三章　以义制利的独家秘诀
Part 3　The Secret of Making an Ethical Profit

105

第四章　传奇商帮的商业伦理
Part 4　Business Ethics of the Legendary Merchant Group

155

第五章　家国天下的晋商风骨
Part 5　The Patriotism of Shanxi Merchants

203

第一章　山西商人的崛起

The Rise of Shanxi Merchants

Part 1.

山西承接东西、连接南北，历史上看是"一带一路"大商圈的重要组成部分。山西特有的地域、文化等因素造就了晋商的开拓创新精神，一代又一代山西商人用他们的智慧与坚韧、气概与谋略，创造了人通天下、货通天下、汇通天下的非凡商业成就。

Historically, Shanxi is an important part of the "the Belt and Road" business circle, connecting the east and west, and connecting the north and south. The unique geographical and cultural factors of Shanxi have nurtured the pioneering and innovative spirit of Shanxi merchants. Generation after generation of Shanxi merchants have created extraordinary commercial achievements with their wisdom, resilience, spirit, and strategy, allowing people, goods, and goods to connect with the world.

一把香料、一勺食盐，在今天的夜宵江湖中，这些廉价的调味品以 C 位出道，俘获了南来北往的食客。但是你知道吗？早在几百年前，它们曾一度占据整个世界商业史的 C 位。

公元 1443 年，当葡萄牙的冒险家们乘着改装的三角帆船，穿越非洲西海岸，雄心勃勃地开辟海上商路时，在欧亚大陆东部，一支中国商队正一路向北、向西，在草原与大漠中走出一条布满艰辛的陆上商路。

历史，竟如此巧合！撬动这两段历史的主角，竟都是我们今天看来毫不起眼的普通调味品。

在中世纪的欧洲，香料的价值堪比黄金，正是对香料的渴望，勾起了人们对东方的向往和对远洋的探索，启动了全球化的最初行动。

在公元 6 世纪的阿比西尼亚王国，盐被当作货币使用，是财富的象征。而在古老的产盐国中国，一个被称为晋商的传奇商帮，因盐致富，开启绵延 500 多年的辉煌，促成了西汉丝绸之路在明清两代的延伸与重建。

Salt and spices are inexpensive but full of flavor, and have captivated diners from everywhere. But hundreds of years ago, these humble condiments dominated commerce around the world.

In 1443, Portuguese adventurers sailed on ambitious maritime trade routes, navigating the western coast of Africa with their triangular caravels. On the eastern reaches of the Eurasian continent, a Chinese trade caravan was heading both north and west. They paved a challenging overland trade route through grasslands and deserts.

History is filled with fascinating coincidences like this. The key players in these two historical chapters were the spices and condiments that we take for granted today.

In medieval Europe, the value of spices was comparable to that of gold. The demand for spices prompted voyages of exploration across the oceans. They were the first steps toward globalization.

In the Kingdom of Abyssinia in the 6th century, salt was a form of currency, and a symbol of wealth. In China, a salt-producing country since ancient times, the legendary Shanxi merchants rose because of salt, and their glory lasted for five centuries. It allowed for the extension and reconstruction of the Western Han Dynasty's Silk Road in the Ming and Qing dynasties.

运城盐池
Yuncheng salt Pond

壹

运城盐池[1]，在长达5000万年的漫长岁月里，它像一只神奇的魔盘，不仅变换着斑斓色彩，还源源不断地析出食盐。盐，是人类最古老的商品之一。这些洁白的晶体，催生财富，凝结着人类智慧，裹挟着历史的尘埃。

公元前8世纪，当世界迈进轴心时代，中国正经历春秋战国的诸侯争霸。居地利之便的晋国，因坐拥运城盐池而国力鼎盛；山西最早的商人猗顿[2]，靠经营盐业而富甲一方，被后人奉为"商贸鼻祖"。在山西，盐自古就是商贸活动中的主角。

公元1368年，明朝建立。为稳固北部边疆，明王朝在长城沿线设置九边重镇，驻扎了数十万大军，可每年庞大的粮草军需，使国库捉襟见肘。

制盐工艺
Salt making technology

❶ 运城盐池：古称河东盐池，因位居黄河以东而得名。它地处晋、陕、豫三省交界处，位于山西省运城市盐湖区，是世界上开发利用最早的盐池之一，有 4600 年以上的开采历史，面积约为 132 平方公里，盐资源储量达到 60 多亿吨，盐分含量高达 80% 以上。

❷ 猗顿：战国初年鲁国人，后因在猗地（今山西运城临猗县）发家致富，殁后又埋葬在猗地，故称猗顿。猗顿对山西南部地区的畜牧业和河东池盐的开发都发挥了十分重要的作用，在山西商业发展史上占着重要的地位。他是山西地区见于史载的最早的大手工业者和大商人，是山西经济史上的重要人物。

《中国万里长城·九边重镇图》
陆沉　贾廷庠　要守文　刘金骅　朱孝忠　李志强　王伟 / 合制
The Great Wall of China and the Nine-Sided City Map
Lu Shen Jia Tingxiang Shou Wen Liu Jinhua Zhu Xiaozhong Li Zhiqiang Wang Wei/combination

❸ 开中法：明代历史上一项非常重要的盐政制度，旨在解决边防卫所驻军所需粮饷而将盐政与边政相结合的一种召商代销制度。《明史·食货志》载："召商输粮而与之盐，谓之开中。"即为了解决戍边将士的军需和粮饷，明政府鼓励商人运送粮草军需到边塞而换取"盐引"。晋商利用自己的地理优势与拥有盐池的自然条件，向大同镇与山西镇运送军需，换取的"盐引"可到指定地点（如河东、长芦、淮浙）领取食盐，再到指定区域销售获得丰厚的利润。山西商人积极输粮贩盐，并逐步扩大经营范围，迅速崛起，开启了晋商持续五百年辉煌的先河。

中国商业史学会会长　王茹芹

据《大明会典》记载：当时边关的辽东、宣府、大同、延绥四个边镇，每年就需要粮食250余万石。250余万石是个什么概念呢？可以养活10多万个家庭，够当时半个南京城的人吃一年。

公元1370年，中书省右丞杨宪向明朝开国皇帝朱元璋上了一道奏折，奏请朝廷鼓励商人给九边重镇运输军粮。而作为交换条件，商人可以换来一纸"盐引"，也就是盐业的经营许可权。这项被称作"开中法"❸的改革如果能够顺利推行，无疑是解了一个大困局，可朱元璋却心存忧虑。

在中国传统农业社会，士、农、工、商一直是社会地位的固定排序，处于末位的商人地位卑贱，即便是在商品经济繁荣的宋代，也被与不孝不悌之徒归为一类，限制衣食住行、不准入仕为官。因此，又有多少人敢无视世俗鄙夷、冲破正统桎梏去经商呢？

然而，朱元璋的担忧，很快就湮没在了长长的军粮运输商队中。"开中法"一经张榜招商，就有不少山西商人把十几万石米粮输纳到边仓。河东盐场顿时商旅穿梭、人声鼎沸，甚至远到江苏两淮盐场与河北长芦盐场，也大多是来自山西的商人。

直到600多年后的今天，依然不断有人向历史追问：面对当年"开中纳粮"的同等机遇，为什么远赴九边经商的大多是山西人？为什么只有山西人顺势而为，创造了日后"海内最富"的奇迹？

站在地理学上400毫米等降水量线的位置上，我们会发现，这条线将土地自然分割成截然不同两种景象：一边半湿润，一边半干旱；一边是森林，一边是草原；一边农耕，一边游牧；一边人口密集，一边地广人稀。

中国人常说，靠天吃饭。如果一个地方的年降水量超不过400毫米，这个地方的人们就无法进行农业种植。所以，400毫米等降水量线，就成了农耕文明的自然极限。在这条线的两侧，形成了气质迥异的两个民族：中原农耕民族和北方游牧民族。矗立在400毫米等降水量线北界的边塞长城，阻隔着游牧民族南下的铁骑，却从来没有妨碍北方与中原的民族交融。它是民族冲突的历史见证，也是民族交往的通道和贸易集散市场。

山西大学经济与管理学院教授　博士生导师　石涛

无论是在任何政治条件下，或者是战争环境下，民间的商业交往是始终存在的。中原地区的手工业制品，在北方少数民族地区深受欢迎，边贸特别繁盛。

山西，素有"表里山河"之称，外有黄河屏障，内有太行山纵横。但"你中有我，我中有你"的民族融合，让山西人骨子里有一种跨越山河阻隔的冲动。所以虽处四塞之地，却不乏纵横四海的眼界魄力和敢为人先的商业基因。历史上的山西，是畅通东西南北的商贸枢纽之地，是"一带一路"大商圈的重要组成部分。

北魏时期，丝绸之路的东方起点就在今天的山西大同，这座当年闻名全球的东方国际大都市，堪比今天的巴黎。隋唐时，大批西域商人，还有从波斯、粟特、天竺等国远道而来的外国使臣和商人，很多是从今天的山西省会太原北上，经蒙古再转道欧洲。他们把带来的宝石、金银器皿卖掉，再把当地的丝绸锦帛带回去，成为古丝绸之路上往来山西的重要客商。13世纪后期，意大利旅行家马可·波罗曾在他的游记中向世界描述他对太原的印象：我从意大利来到中国，游历到太原府，发现这里商业相当发达，葡萄园非常多，酿出的葡萄酒被贩运到契丹各处不产酒的地方。

在频繁的商贸往来中，山西商人构建起遍布全国的商业物流网络，打通了小到针头线脑、大到棉粮物资的丰富货源渠道。这些网络与渠道在"开中纳粮"商机到来时，成为山西商人抢占先机、输粮纳盐的重要优势。

皮影戏：马可·波罗对话胡人吃饼骑驼俑
Shadow puppet: Marco Polo talks to a Hu man eating bread and riding a camel

山西省晋商文化研究会常务理事　张宪平

其实，纳粮换盐引并非是很容易做的买卖，因为这里边的商业风险是难以预料的，比如政策变化、手中的盐引不能及时兑现等等，也就是说要求经营者不但要具备精明的商业头脑，而且要具备能够承担巨大商业风险的胆量。就是在别人犹豫的时候，晋商紧紧抓住了这个机遇，顺势而为，完成了自己的原始资本积累，拉开了他们建立自己商业帝国的序幕。

"开中法"犹如一根有力的杠杆，撬动了山西人行商天下的敏感神经。越来越多的山西人走出家门，他们从不安享小富、止步于大胜，而是策马扬鞭，开启一段又一段更广阔的征程。

1

Over the course of a staggering 50 million years, Yuncheng Salt Lake's ever-changing kaleidoscope has continuously yielded crystalline salt. Salt is one of humanity's oldest commodities. These immaculate white crystals have created wealth. They are the embodiment of wisdom and history.

In the 8th century BC, China experienced the upheavals of the Spring and Autumn period and the Warring States period. The State of Jin wielded power due to its control of the Yuncheng Salt Lake. Yi Dun, Shanxi's earliest merchant, accumulated huge wealth by running the salt business, and is regarded as the founder of commerce and trade. Since ancient times, salt has always played a leading role in Shanxi's commercial activities.

In 1368, the Ming Dynasty was established. To secure the northern frontier, nine military strongholds were set up along the Great Wall, and hundreds of thousands of troops were stationed there. The enormous amount of provisions needed for them strained the state treasury.

> **WANG RUQIN, PRESIDENT**
> **SOCIETY OF CHINESE COMMERCE HISTORY**
> According to the records of the Collected Statutes of the Ming Dynasty, at that time, Liaodong, Xuanfu, Datong, and Yansui these four border towns required over 2.5 million dan of grain each year. What does that number mean? It could feed more than 100,000 families, enough to sustain half of Nanjing's population in the Ming Dynasty for a year.

In 1370, Yang Xian, right chancellor of the Central Secretariat, presented a memorial to the Ming's founding emperor Zhu Yuanzhang. He asked the court to encourage merchants to transport military provisions to the nine military strongholds along the border. In exchange, these merchants would obtain a document known as a "Salt Certificate", granting them the right to engage in the salt industry.

This reform was known as the "Kai Zhong Law", and offered a solution to a major dilemma. However, the emperor had his concerns.

In the traditional agricultural society in China, the four classes of people, namely scholars, farmers, artisans and merchants, had fixed social standing. Merchants were at the bottom. Even in the Song Dynasty when the commodity economy boomed, they were still thought to be unfilial and undutiful individuals, and subjected to various restrictions on clothing, food, housing, and travel. They were also forbidden from holding official positions. So, few would dare to defy social taboos and engage in commerce.

However, the emperor quickly forgot these concerns when he saw the long lines of caravans bringing provisions to the military. When the Kai Zhong Law was announced, many Shanxi merchants delivered large amounts of grain to the border warehouses. The Hedong Saltworks became a bustling hub filled with merchants. Even the Lianghuai Saltworks far away in Jiangsu and the Changlu Saltworks in Hebei were filled with merchants from Shanxi.

Even today, more than 600 years on, people still asked. Why were Shanxi merchants the first to respond to the Kai Zhong Law and venture into the nine military strongholds for trade? When everyone had the same policy opportunities, why did Shanxi merchants become "the richest in the country"?

Drawing a line with our current location, one side is semi-humid while the other is semi-arid; one side features forests while the other is covered in grasslands; one side practices agriculture while the other follows nomadic traditions; one side has dense populations while the other is sparsely populated. This line, distinctly dividing this land into two contrasting landscapes, is known as the 400-millimeter isohyet in geography.

There is a saying in China that farmers depend on Heaven for food. If the annual precipitation in an area is no higher than 400 millimeters, people cannot work their fields. Thus, this isohyet became the natural threshold for agricultural civilization. On either side of the line, two distinctly different ethnic groups thrived, the farmers in the Central Plains and the nomadic tribes in the North.

Standing at the northern border of the isohyet is the Great Wall, which served as a barrier against the cavalries of the nomadic tribes. However, this has never hindered the fusion of the ethnic groups of the North and the Central Plains. It's a historical witness to both ethnic conflicts and a corridor of commerce between different ethnicities.

> **PROF. SHI TAO,**
> **DOCTORAL SUPERVISOR, SCHOOL OF ECONOMICS**
> **AND MANAGEMENT, SHANXI UNIVERSITY**
> In any political context, and even during periods of conflict, interactions among the people, especially the commercial interactions, still existed. The handicraft products from the Central Plains gained popularity in the northern minority regions, fostering a flourishing border trade.

Shanxi has the Yellow River as a barrier on the outside and the Taihang Mountains on the inside. But its ethnic integration has given Shanxi people a congenital impulse to stride across the mountains and rivers. As a result, although they are born in a place surrounded by natural barriers, they never lack the vision to see the world or the spirit of being commercial pioneers.

In history, Shanxi served as a pivotal hub for commerce and trade, and was an essential part of the "Belt and Road" commercial network.

During the Northern Wei period, the eastern starting point of the Silk Road was situated in present-day Datong, an oriental cosmopolis that rivalled today's Paris in importance. In the Sui and Tang Dynasties, many merchants from the Western Regions, as well as foreign envoys and traders from places like Persia, Sogdia and India, traveled to Shanxi's capital, Taiyuan, and then north to Europe through Mongolia. In the late 13th century, the Italian explorer Marco Polo described his impressions of Taiyuan to the world.

Marco Polo: I traveled from Italy to China and ventured to Taiyuan Prefecture, where I found the business was flourishing. There were numerous vineyards producing abundant grape wine. This wine is traded and transported to various places of the Khitan, where wine is not locally produced.

Merchants from the Western Regions: If we are talking about exploring Shanxi, I was here over 700 years before you. We the caravan from the Western Regions, arrived in ancient Jinyang in the 6th century. We sold precious gemstones, gold and silver vessels, and in return, we took back local silk and brocade. We were important merchants on the ancient Silk Road, traveling to and from Shanxi.

In their frequent commercial activities, Shanxi merchants established a logistics network covering the entire country, opening up extensive supply channels for both petty and major commodities. These channels later became an important advantage which enabled them to quickly respond to the Kai Zhong Law.

ZHANG XIANPING, MANAGING DIRECTOR
SHANXI MERCHANTS CULTURE RESEARCH
ASSOCIATION OF SHANXI PROVINCE

Transporting military provisions to exchange for the Salt Certificate was not an easy business, as it involved unpredictable risks. For example, the policy might change and the Salt Certificate might not be cashed out. So, the operators must have both business acumen and the courage to take huge risks. When others were still hesitating, Shanxi merchants seized the opportunity and completed their primary accumulation of capital, which was the prelude to the building of a great commercial empire.

The Kai Zhong Law came as a powerful incentive for the Shanxi people. More and more of them left their hometown for a bigger world. They did not settle for just modest prosperity, but set forth on even broader journeys, seeking new horizons time and time again.

大型历史实景剧《走西口》
Large-scale historical reality drama "Go West"

一首凄美的《走西口》，唱得让历史垂泪。

就是这些擦一把眼泪狠心踏出家门的山西男儿，凭着开拓进取精神，白手起家，不惧艰难险阻，开辟万里茶道，创建中国票号，成为一座城市、一种商业文明的缔造者。他们当中，就有祁县乔家的先祖乔贵发和榆次常家先祖常威。

位于山西北部的雁门关，是万里长城的重要关口。它以"险"著称，被誉为"中华第一关"。出了雁门关往北再走100里，有一个叫"黄花梁"的地方，在这个地方有一个岔路口，一条路通往张家口，一条路通往杀虎口。

"杀虎口"实景还原
"Kill tiger Mouth" real scene restoration

据说当年背井离乡走西口❶的山西人，其实他们并不知道到底应该往东走还是往西走，所以就在一个岔路口抛鞋择路。鞋头朝左"走西口"，鞋头朝右"走东口"，用一只鞋子下一次豪赌，赌的是生存的希望，是更广阔的生命空间。

从这个岔口出发，祁县农民乔贵发一路向西，帮人拉骆驼打零工。他靠着省吃俭用攒下的本钱，在包头城开了间豆腐坊。豆腐坊的生意越做越红火，可乔贵发却有了更大的盘算。面对同行的激烈竞争，他果断转型，率先干起了"买树梢"❷的粮食期货，狠狠地赚了一笔。

初次转型首战告捷，更坚定了他多业经营、跨界发展的商业理想。卖

张家口大境门
Zhangjiakou Dajing Gate

❶ 走西口：明清时期，山西、陕西等地民众前往长城以外的内蒙古草原垦荒、经商的活动被称为"走西口"。当时，由于山西等地人口增长、土地贫瘠、自然灾害频繁等原因，人们为了谋求更好的生活，纷纷前往口外的蒙古地区。走西口的路线主要有两条，一条是从山西杀虎口，一条是从陕西府谷口。走西口的人群不仅带去了农耕技术，促进了当地的农业发展，也推动了蒙汉之间的经济、文化交流。

❷ 买树梢：山西商人的一种以预购为特色的经营模式。春天预先以商定的较低价格订购尚未挂果的树梢的收成，由于秋天实际收成存在不确定性，这有助于降低农户的经营风险，同时商人也可以因此有较多获利。这种经营方式被形象地称作"买树梢"，与"买青苗"类似。买树梢实际上是一种商业与金融相结合的经营模式。

草料、开油坊、开当铺，经过几代人的努力，凭着吃苦耐劳、艰苦创业的精神，乔家的店铺从内蒙古拓展到了东北、西北等地的主要商业城市，资产高达千万两白银，成为明清晋商的一代翘楚。

> **中国商业史学会会长　王茹芹**
> 山西商人到包头经商，杀虎口是必经之路。当时有句民谣是这样唱的："杀虎口，杀虎口，没有钱财难过口，不是丢钱财，就是刀砍头，过了虎口心还抖。"但是，像乔贵发这样的山西商人从来没有退却，走出去的人也越来越多。

当乔贵发在包头城经营豆腐坊时，他的老乡、榆次常家的常威父子在张家口创立的"大德玉"杂货店已颇具规模。当年，站在"黄花梁"岔路口的常威，并没有"抛鞋择路"，而是受人指点选择了"走东口"。常氏祖先以耕种畜牧为业，历经七代人积累，到第八代常威时，已经不愁温饱，但他并不满足于"老婆孩子热炕头"的小日子。公元1681年，年仅20岁的常威肩上披着褡裢，里面装着占卜用的摇桶和六枚铜钱，靠着一路行医打卦走到了张家口摆摊卖布。经过数十年积累、两代人接力，等到常威告老还乡时，常家已在张家口设立了"大德常"和"大德玉"两大字号。

俄国作家阿·马·波兹德涅耶夫在旅行日记中记下了公元1892年在张家口的所见所闻："在元宝山谷地的崖坡上，鳞次栉比地排列着货品充盈的商铺，它们的老板主要是和到张家口来的蒙古人做买卖的北京商人和老醯儿商人。"

常威的儿子常万达在与俄蒙商人做生意的过程中发现,俄罗斯人对中国的茶叶非常痴迷,尤其对武夷山红茶情有独钟。所以,常万达决定把张家口的"大德玉"总部迁到中俄边境,开展对俄茶叶贸易,并倾囊而出,踏上开辟"万里茶道"的漫漫征程。

如果说,当年山西商人开中纳盐是因为坐拥资源之便,那么今天迈出这一步,却是一条无中生有、充满未知的冒险之路。世上本没有路,走的人多了就成了路。这个常家最小的儿子,从此走出了父辈的目光,走向一个超越中国版图的更大的世界。

雁门关　Yanmen Pass

2

The sad ballad, Going Out of the Xikou Pass, has been known to move people to tears.

It was these Shanxi men who wiped away their tears and stepped out of the house ruthlessly. With their pioneering spirit, they started from scratch, not afraid of difficulties and obstacles, opened up Wanli Tea Road, created a Chinese ticket number, and became the creators of a city and a commercial civilization. Among them, there are Qiao Guifa, the ancestor of the Qiao family in Qixian County, and Chang Wei, the ancestor of the Chang family in Yuci.

Located in the northern part of Shanxi, Yanmen Pass is a crucial gateway of the Great Wall. It is renowned for its treacherous terrain and has been dubbed the "No. 1 Pass in China". 50km north of Yanmen Pass lies a place called Huanghua Ridge. Here it is. At this juncture, there's a crossroad, one path leads to Zhangjiakou, and the other leads to Shahu Pass.

Legend has it that when the Shanxi people went out of the Xikou Pass to seek their fortune, they were unsure whether to go east or west. So, at this crossroad, they tossed a shoe, to guide their path and make the decision for them.

If the shoe's toe pointed left, they would go west. If it pointed right, they would go east. It was a bold gamble. This gamble was about their hope for better livelihood and broader space.

Begining this crossroad, Qiao Guifa, a farmer from Qixian County, headed west. He made his living as a camel puller. He used his savings to open a tofu mill in the city of Baotou. The business of the mill thrived, but Qiao Guifa had greater ambition. Facing the fierce competition in the industry, he decisively switched to grain futures and made a big fortune.

The successful business transformation made him even more determined to engage in different industries. His family sold fodder, and set up oil mills and pawnshops. With the efforts by several generations, the stores of the Qiao family expanded from Inner Mongolia to major commercial cities in Northeast China and northwestern China, with total assets worth tens of millions of taels of silver. The Qiao family became prominent among the Shanxi merchants in the Ming and Qing Dynasties.

> **WANG RUQIN, PRESIDENT**
> **SOCIETY OF CHINESE COMMERCE HISTORY**
>
> In the past, when Shanxi merchants did business in Baotou, they had to pass through the Shahu Pass. There was a folk song that went, "Shahu Pass, Shahu Pass, without money, it's hard to get by; you may lose your wealth or even lose your life. Even after crossing the pass, your heart still trembles. " However, Shanxi merchants like Qiao Guifa did not give up, and an increasing number of them ventured out into the world.

While Qiao Guifa ran his tofu mill in Baotou, his fellow villagers Chang Wei and his son from the Chang family in Yuci had already established a sizeable Dadeyu variety store in Zhangjiakou. 50 years ago, standing at the crossroad of Huanghua Ridge Chang Wei made a decision to go east.

In the Chang ancestral house, a shepherd's shovel is always on display. Across seven generations, the Chang ancestors toiled in farming and husbandry, amassing enough wealth so that the eighth generation, represented by Chang Wei, no longer struggled just to survive. Yet, Chang Wei yearned for broader horizons.

This is a bag with a pocket at both ends, called "Shaoma" or "Dalian". Back then, Chang Wei set forth from his home with a bag like this over his shoulder.

In 1681, the 20th year of the Qing Emperor Kangxi's reign, the 20-year-old Chang Wei traveled to Zhangjiakou, where he set up a cloth stall using his skills in traditional medicine and fortune-telling. After decades of hard work and the efforts of two generations, by the time Chang Wei returned to his hometown, the Chang family had established two prominent trade names in Zhangjiakou, Dadechang and Dadeyu.

This footage captures the bustling scene outside the Dajing Gate of Zhangjiakou in 1928. Camel caravans were being prepared for long and arduous journeys. Russian writer A. M. Pozdneev noted in his travel diary what he saw in Zhangjiakou in 1892. "On the cliffs of Yuanbao Mountain Valley, shops with abundant merchandise stand in rows, primarily owned by Beijing and Shanxi merchants who come to Zhangjiakou for trade."

Chang Wanda, the son of Chang Wei, discovered during his business dealings with Russian and Mongolian traders that Russians loved Chinese tea, particularly the black tea from Wuyi Mountain. Encouraged by this, Chang Wanda made a bold decision to relocate the Dadeyu headquarters from Zhangjiakou to the border of China and Russia with no effort spared and began an arduous journey to build the Tea Road.

While the salt trade in the past was based on the advantage provided local resources, this step was filled with unknown risks and adventures. As one saying goes, "The earth had no roads to begin with, but when many men pass one way, a road is made. "This youngest son of the Chang family stepped out of his ancestors' shadow and ventured beyond China's boundaries, forging a path into a larger realm.

寻踪
晋商

鄱阳湖老爷庙
Poyang Lake master temple

叁

　　鄱阳湖老爷庙水域，被称为中国的"百慕大"。千百年来，在这里失踪的船只不计其数，甚至有载重 2000 多吨的大船也在此沉没。而当年的山西商人，若想从福建贩茶北上恰克图交易，这片凶险的水域就是必经之路。

　　公元 1885 年，《资本论》第二卷在伦敦出版。马克思在书中记录下了这条由中国商人开辟的、长达 13000 里的"万里茶道"❶："茶叶由陆路用骆驼和牛车运抵边防要塞长城边上的张家口，再从那里经过草原或沙漠、大戈壁，越过 1282 俄里到达恰克图……"

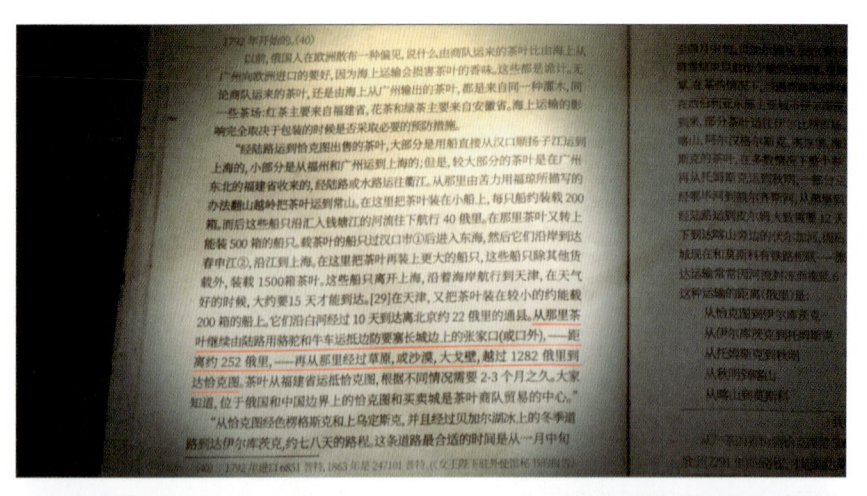

《资本论》第二卷

Das Kapital Volume two

❶ 万里茶道：自 17 世纪末开始，伴随着俄罗斯市场对茶叶需求的不断增加和中俄茶叶贸易的逐渐兴盛，以大盛魁商号为领头羊的晋商抓住机遇，贯通了南起武夷山、北达俄罗斯圣彼得堡的茶叶贸易之路，这条长达 13000 里的贸易通道被称作万里茶道。如今，随着中蒙俄三国携手共建"一带一路"，这条曾经的"世纪动脉"的历史文化价值被不断重新发现，在推动经贸合作、促进民心相通的时代浪潮里焕发出新的生机。

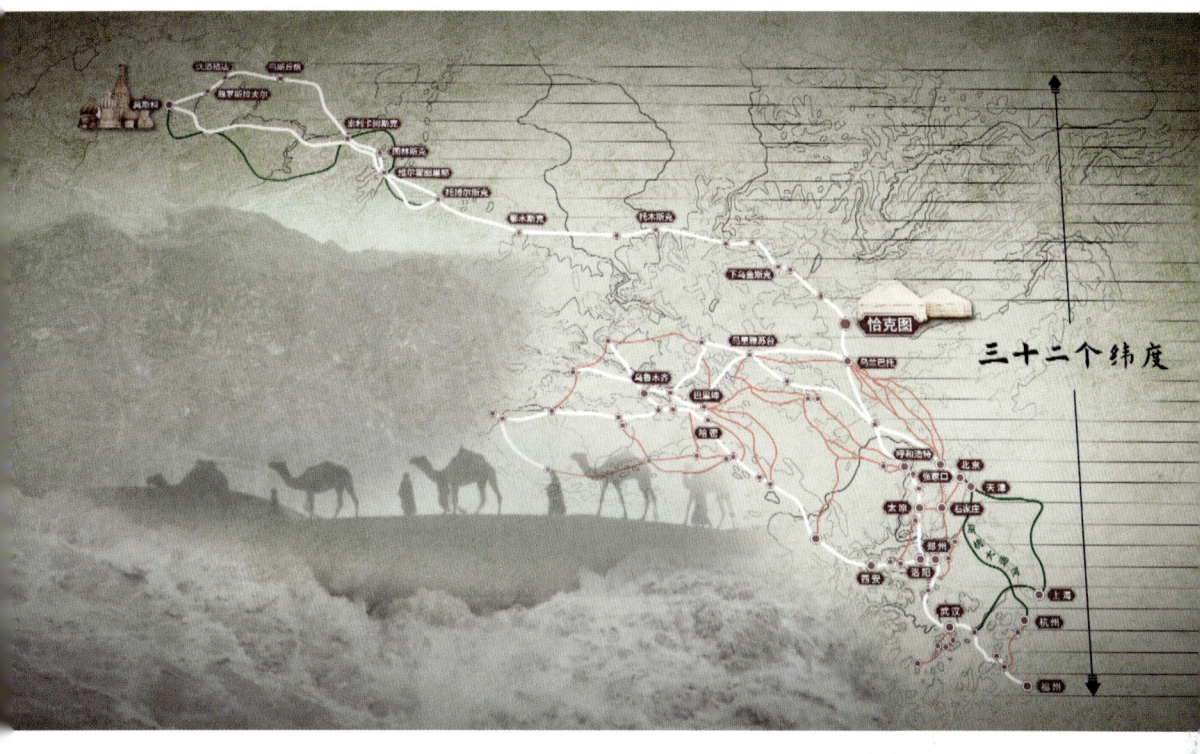

跨越三十二个纬度的万里茶道
A tea ceremony spanning 32 latitudes

从中国的福建、湖南、湖北等产茶地到达陆路口岸恰克图，再出境运往俄罗斯，从南到北跨越 32 个纬度，除了激流险滩，还有崇山峻岭、戈壁荒原。

美国籍媒体评论员　托马斯·鲍肯二世

商人们必须应对不同的天气条件、地形地貌等，尤其是在中国北部或西北部地区，夏日绵长、冬夜漫漫，有很多狼，它们成群结队地行动，商人们不得不团结在一起。

浑善达克沙漠
The Hunshandak Desert

张家口市文物考古研究所副研究员
中国万里茶道专业委员会委员　李现云

浑善达克沙漠，是张家口到库伦的必经之路，夏天的时候，气温可以高达四五十度，到了冬天又可以达到零下四五十度。对于商人来说是，走沙漠就相当于要面对冰与火的考验。

张库大道历史文化研究会常务理事　侯权民

当年商人们走到这里的时候，经常是黄沙满天，很容易迷失方向。

公元1758年春天，常万达的驼队在前往库伦途中遭遇了一场沙尘暴，驼队在沙漠里迷失了方向，被困多日找不到水源。就在大家瘫倒在沙漠中身陷绝境时，常万达骑了多年的一峰雄驼突然站起来挣脱缰绳。

张库大道历史博物馆馆长　刘振瑛

骆驼要挣扎着跑，小伙计赶紧拽住缰绳，常万达一看，说："得了，都到了这个时候了，你把缰绳松开吧，多活一个算一个，让它走吧。"小伙计解下了缰绳，这个骆驼起身以后，向沙坡底下走去，翻上了一个沙梁以后，没有跑掉，回头鸣叫。骆驼到了沟底就开始刨这个沙地，用掌刨，常万达说："这儿肯定有水，大家努努力。"大家一起下去以后拼命地挖，最后，终于挖出了一眼泉水。

一峰骆驼、一汪泉水，救了一支数十人的商队。回程时常万达特意拉来几块木板，在泉边围起了一口井。在此后的岁月里，多少南来北往的商队，靠着这口"救命井"在沙漠中死里逃生。

张库大道历史博物馆馆长　刘振瑛

从库伦到恰克图，这段路不是很长，但是经常会碰到匪帮。由于语言不通，所以一见面，必须是真刀真枪地干，要不你杀死他，要不他杀死你。所以说，这条路是非常悲壮的一条路。

山西大学经济与管理学院教授　博士生导师　石涛

成功的商人实际上是非常有限的。更多走出去的山西商人，客死他乡的、埋骨荒漠的非常多。

恰克图与买卖城
Kyakhta and the city of Trade

　　敢走别人不敢走的路，能吃别人吃不了的苦。在榆次常家的家谱中，从九世常万达一辈至十三世，396 名男子中有 39 人因外出经商而客死他乡。历尽艰险的山西商人，终于在中国地图上走出了一条从张家口大境门出发，途经库伦，再通往恰克图的商道。他们用一片茶叶，点燃了中俄一万多公里冰雪疆界上的沸腾生活。

　　300 米宽的中俄边境线，两条木栅栏隔开一北一南两处聚集区。北面地处当时的俄国境内，叫恰克图，因为在俄语中，恰克图的意思，就是"有茶的地方"；南面在当时的中国境内，因为居住的大多是山西商人，而山西人又习惯把"贸易"称为"买卖"，所以久而久之，就被叫成了

"买卖城"。

甘肃政法大学丝路法学院俄罗斯籍教授　奥莉娅

买卖城和恰克图是那个时代的贸易战略城市,这两个城市相对而立,在它们之间有一条非常狭窄的地带,我们称之为"无人区"。而恰恰是这个地方,给俄罗斯西伯利亚地区和中国地区都带来了发展,商品不断通过这些城市,从中国运来,这要归功于晋商在西伯利亚开设了大量的商店。

恰克图从不毛之地变成了一个商埠重镇。公元1793年8月,英国使团不远万里来到中国,向80多岁的乾隆皇帝觐献了一个精美的地球仪,他们收到的回赠礼品,则是中国砖茶。一赠一回,未曾提前沟通,却如此心意相通。此时,中国人脚下的"万里茶道",已从当时俄国境内一直向西延伸,辐射到中亚和欧洲腹地。

山西财经大学晋商研究院副院长　乔南

万里茶道是明清时期对古丝绸之路的一种重构或者重建,延展或者开发。

大益集团法国籍国际交流专员　孙博

在这条路上,这些商人贩运茶叶,沿着这条路,一直到俄罗斯莫

杀虎口
Cut the jaws of a tiger

斯科、圣彼得堡,一直行进到欧洲,像丝绸之路一样。这些商人还增进了各国之间的联系,促进了途经各国之间文化、外交、经济和人文的交流。

明清两代、数百年间,成千上万的山西商人汇入"丝绸之路"的滚滚洪流。他们走到哪里就把财富带到哪里,把文明的种子播撒到哪里,把曾经被山遥路远而阻隔的世界联结到一起。一曲《走西口》,奏响了欧亚大陆商贸流通、世界经济文化交流的宏大乐章。

3

The Laoyemiao Waters in Poyang Lake are known as China's Bermuda Triangle. Over the centuries, countless ships have been vanished here. Even vessels weighing over 2,000 tons have sunk in these waters. In the past, when Shanxi merchants went northward from Fujian to trade in Kyakhta, they had to pass through the treacherous waters here.

In 1885, volume two of Das Kapital was published in London. In it, Marx mentioned the Tea Road, spanning over 6,500km, pioneered by Chinese merchants. "Tea leaves were transported by land using camels and ox wagons to Zhangjiakou, the border fortress of the Great Wall. From there, they crossed grasslands, deserts, and the vast Gobi Desert, traveling over 1,282 versts to reach Kyakhta..."

The journey started from tea-producing regions in China such as Fujian, Hunan, and Hubei. It led to Kyakhta, a land port, and then onward to Russia. This extensive route spanned 32 latitudes from south to north, bringing merchants through treacherous rapids, steep mountains, and barren deserts.

> **PAUKEN II THOMAS WEIR, AMERICAN COMMENTATOR**
> You have to deal with major weather conditions, the terrain and like, especially in northern or northwestern China, has very long summers, very long winters, had many wolves in this area. They traveled around and packed. So a lot of the merchants had to stick together.

The Hunshandake Sandland was a place that had to be passed from

Zhangjiakou to Kulun. Here, the temperatures in summer can reach as high as 40 to 50 degrees Celsius and the temperatures in winter can drop to minus 40 to 50 degrees Celsius. For traders, trekking in the desert was like a journey through ice and fire.

In the spring of 1758, while on their way to Kulun, Chang Wanda's camel caravan got caught in a fierce sandstorm. They were lost in the desert for days and unable to find any water source. As everyone lay exhausted in the desert, Chang's loyal camel suddenly stood up and broke free from its reins.

The camel struggled to run, yet a young man hurriedly grabbed the reins. Chang Wanda noticed and said, "Just release the reins. It's good if it can survive. Let it go. "So, the young man released its reins. After the camel stood up, it walked toward the foot of the sand slope, then it turned back and called out, instead of running away. As soon as it reached the bottom of the gully, it began digging into the sand with its hooves. Chang Wanda said, "There must be water here. Let's put in some effort. " They dug together, and eventually found a spring.

One camel and a spring saved a caravan of dozens of people. On their return journey, Chang brought several pieces of wood and fenced around the spring. In the years that followed, countless trading caravans relied on this "lifesaving well" to survive in the desert.

> **LIU ZHENYING, CURATOR**
> ***ZHANGJIAKOU-KULUN ROUTE HISTORY MUSEUM***
> The camel struggled to run, yet a young man hurriedly grabbed the reins. Chang Wanda noticed and said, "Just release the reins. It's good if it can survive. Let it go. "So, the young man released its reins. After the camel stood up, it walked toward the foot of the sand slope, then it turned back and called out, instead of running away. As soon as it reached the bottom of the gully, it

began digging into the sand with its hooves. Chang Wanda said, "There must be water here. Let's put in some effort. " They dug together, and eventually found a spring.

PROF. SHI TAO, DOCTORAL SUPERVISOR
SCHOOL OF ECONOMICS AND MANAGEMENT, SHANXI UNIVERSITY
Successful merchants were actually quite few. Many Shanxi merchants who ventured out from Shanxi met their ends in foreign lands or got buried in desert.

They went where others wouldn't dare and endured hardships others couldn't bear. From the ninth generation of the Chang family represented by Chang Wanda, to the thirteenth generation, there were 396 men. 39 of them died far away from home while on trading expeditions.

Shanxi merchants, having endured all kinds of hardships, finally paved out a trade route starting from Zhangjiakou, passing Kulun and ending at Kyakhta. Along the icy border of over 10, 000km between China and Russia, tea ignited a bustling life.

The 300-meter-wide border was divided by two wooden fences into two areas. On the northern side lies Kyakhta of Russian. Kyakhta means a place with tea in the Russian language. The southern side, which was within China's territory at the time, was inhabited mostly by Shanxi merchants, who referred to trade as "buying and selling, "thus giving the place the name "Buy-and-sell City".

PRONKINA OLGA, RUSSIAN PROFESSOR
SILK ROAD LAW SCHOOL OF GANSU UNIVERSITY OF
POLITICAL SCIENCE AND LAW

The Buy-and-sell City and Kyakhta were strategic hubs of commerce during that era. Situated in close proximity, separated by a narrow strip known as the "no man's land", these two cities played a vital role. These two places contributed to the development of both the Siberian region of Russia and China. Goods continually flowed from China to Russia through these cities, which owed much to the numerous shops set up by Shanxi merchants in Siberia.

The thriving of trade transformed Kyakhta from a place of barren land into a bustling port town. In August 1793, a British delegation traveled to China and presented an exquisite globe to the 80-year-old Emperor Qianlong. In return, they received a Chinese tea brick as a gift.

The exchange of gifts demonstrated a remarkable sense of mutual understanding. At this time, the Tea Road travelled by the Chinese people had extended westward from within Russia to Central Asia and the heartlands of Europe.

QIAO NAN, DEPUTY DEAN
INSTITUTE OF SHANXI MERCHANT STUDIES
SHANXI UNIVERSITY OF FINANCE AND ECONOMICS

The Tea Road should be considered a reconstruction or revival, an extension or development of the ancient Silk Road during the Ming and Qing dynasties.

寻踪
晋商

JULIEN BONZON
FRENCH INTERNATIONAL EXCHANGE SPECIALIST,
TAETEA GROUP

On this road, these merchants traded and transported tea. They traveled along the road all the way to Russia, to Moscow, to Saint Petersburg, and to Europe in the end, just like the Silk Road. These merchants also brought the countries closer together, and promoted cultural, diplomatic and economic communications between all the countries along the road.

For centuries during the Ming and Qing Dynasties, countless Shanxi merchants embraced the surging popularity of the Silk Road. Wherever they went, they brought Wherever they went, they brought wealth and spread the seeds of civilization, connecting distant worlds previously separated by mountains and vast distances.

The song Going Out of the Xikou Pass resounded with the grand symphony of Eurasian commerce as well as global economic and cultural exchanges.

寻踪晋商

平遥古城全景
Panoramic view of Pingyao Ancient City

肆

126 年前，在上海外滩 6 号诞生了中国第一家现代银行——中国通商银行。不过它还有一个名气非常大的"乡下外祖父"——日昇昌票号[1]，比它早出生了 74 年。

19 世纪初的一天，山西平遥西裕成颜料庄的二少爷李大全在街头偶遇一个"看宝盆"的伙计。"看宝盆"，就是在赌客手中的色子落地时给大伙儿报点数。这个伙计机敏过人，色子一落地，瞅一眼就能精准地算出点数。这次偶然的相遇，竟在数年之后创造了一段百年辉煌的金融传奇。

这个伙计名叫雷履泰，后来被李大全任命为西裕成颜料庄京都分号的领班，可他的商业才华远不止于对数字的敏感。有一次，李大全一位在天津做生意的朋友想带着银子去北京，为了避免运输麻烦，就把银子存到了西裕成天津分号，再开具收款证明，拿着证明到北京分号取银子。这个不经意的人情往来，却让雷履泰捕捉到了一个巨大的商机。

用一张汇票取代起镖运现，商家只要拿着一张汇票就能在全国各地自由贸易。雷履泰的这套异地兑现业务，在古老的中国开创了一种全新的金融业态。公元 1823 年，西裕成颜料庄改组成"日昇昌"票号，雷履泰也成为中国票号业的"开山鼻祖"。

[1] 日昇昌票号：平遥"西裕成"财东李大全于公元 1823 年出资 30 万两银改颜料庄为票号，取名"日昇昌"，即取其"旭日初升，繁荣昌盛"之意。日昇昌票号是中国第一家专营存款、放款、汇兑业务的私人金融机构，辉煌时分号遍布全国 30 多个城市、乡镇，甚至远及东南亚、欧美，以"汇通天下"著称于世。

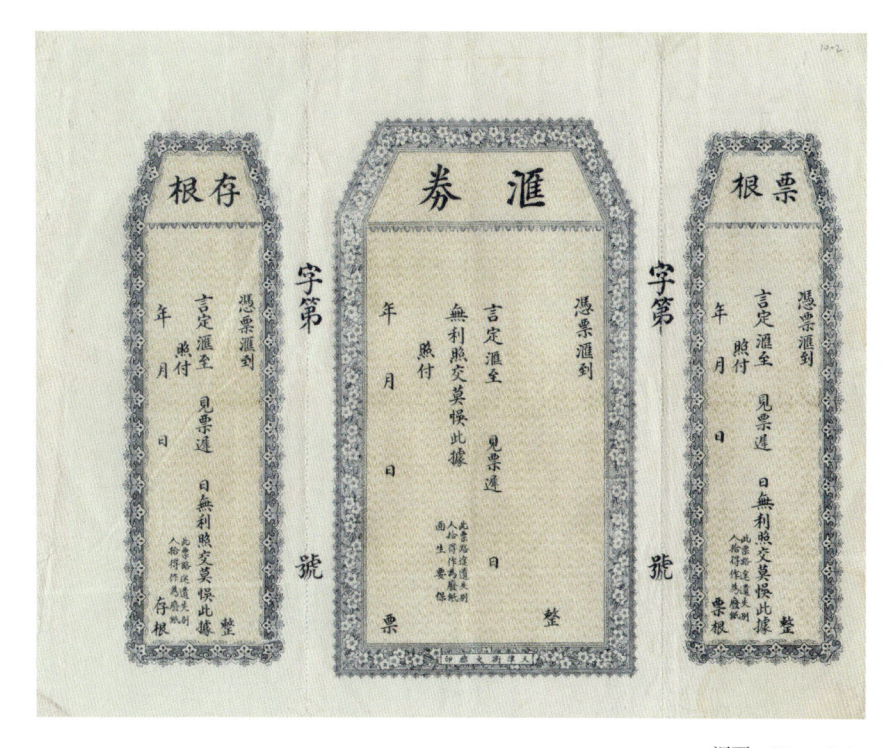

汇票　Money Order

中国商业史学会会长　王茹芹

> 凭一张汇票就可以实现异地存取白银，这是晋商独到的智慧。山西商人的活动不仅在国内，还在国外，当时在俄罗斯、新加坡、日本都可以实现一张汇票"汇通天下"。

卸下了实银运送的重担，东西南北的金融脉络很快通畅起来，在将近一个世纪里，山西商人几乎垄断了全国的金融业务。据考证：公元1881年，仅在汉口就有33家分号。"执中国金融之牛耳"的山西商人，创造

會券

憑票收滙到
永茂長寶號兌貳現捌寶銀壹仟貳佰兩
定會到西口明四月標本號見票照數
無利交還勿悞此據

汇通天下牌匾
Huitong world plaque

性地推动了商业资本与金融资本在中国的融合。甲午战争后，山西商人的票号还开到了日本，跨越国界的商业流通，也被一纸汇票激活。就连中国近代名人梁启超先生都称"颇以票号为荣"。

当代作家余秋雨曾在他的书中这样评价山西商人："人们可以称赞他们'随机应变'，但对'机'的发现，正是由于视野的开阔、目光的敏锐。"晋商"纵横欧亚九千里，称雄商界五百年"。开拓进取、自强不息、不畏艰辛、敢于冒险。而这些熠熠闪光的优秀品质也是中华民族优秀传统文化的精神根脉。

4

126 years ago, at No. 6 the Bund, Shanghai, the first modern bank in China was born, the Imperial Bank of China. But do you know that it had an equally famous "countryside grandfather" that predated it Rishengchang private bank by 74 years?

Li Daquan was a young master of the Xiyucheng Pigment Shop in Pingyao, Shanxi, in the early 19th century. One day, he encountered a clever assistant on the street who could accurately predict the outcome of dice. This assistant was quick-witted and could instantly calculate the points as soon as the dice landed.

This chance encounter led to the creation of a legend in the history of finance.

This assistant's name was Lei Lvtai, and he was later appointed by Li Daquan as the head of the Beijing branch of the Xiyucheng Pigment Shop. However, his business talent extended far beyond being sensitive to numbers. On one occasion, one of Li Daquan's friends who did business in Tianjin wanted to take silver to Beijing. To avoid the hassle of transportation, he decided to deposit the silver at the Tianjin branch of Xiyucheng and asked Li Daquan to issue a receipt. Armed with this receipt, he would then go to the Beijing branch to withdraw the silver. This seemingly casual transaction opened Lei Lvtai's eyes to a tremendous business opportunity.

By replacing the dangerous traditional system with a single promissory note, businessmen could now engage in free trade across the country by simply presenting this note. Lei Lvtai's pioneering cross-regional exchange business introduced an entirely new form of finance to ancient China. In 1823, Xiyucheng Pigment Shop became Rishengchang private bank, and Lei Lvtai became the "founding father" of China's banking industry.

> **WANG RUQIN, PRESIDENT**
> **SOCIETY OF CHINESE COMMERCE HISTORY**
> The ability to access silver in different locations with just a single promissory note was the result of the unique wisdom of Shanxi merchants. Some of their activities extended beyond China's borders. They were able to "connect the world" with a single piece of paper, even in far-off places like Russia, Singapore, and Japan.

Relieved of the burden of transporting physical silver, financial networks everywhere were soon unimpeded. Shanxi merchants virtually monopolized the country's financial sector for nearly a century. In 1881 alone, there were 33 branches in Hankou. The Shanxi merchants held the "reins of Chinese finance", and creatively brought about the integration of commercial and financial capital in China. After the First Sino-Japanese War, Shanxi merchants even expanded their private banks to Japan and cross-border business could be done with a single promissory note. Even the modern Chinese figure, Liang Qichao, regarded them with pride.

Contemporary writer Yu Qiuyu once praised Shanxi merchants by saying, "People may admire their adaptability, but the discovery of these 'opportunities' was precisely due to their broad vision and keen insight."

We say that the Shanxi merchants did business across Eurasia and dominated the business world of China for five centuries. They were pioneering, unyielding, fearless, and willing to take risks. These qualities are the spiritual foundation of the outstanding traditional culture of the Chinese nation.

因盐而起、因茶而兴、因票号而至鼎盛辉煌。风雨 500 年，一代又一代山西商人用他们的智慧与坚韧、气概与谋略，走出了一条横跨欧亚大陆的经济文化大通道，一条长达 5150 公里的漫漫茶路，一条"汇通天下"的传奇之路。

视野有多大，胸怀就有多大！

这些"海内最富"的山西商人，留给后人的财富，不仅仅是一座座豪宅大院，他们万里驰骋探索未知世界的传奇故事，更是在茫茫史海响绝尘音。

纪录片《寻踪晋商》第一集：
《山西商人的崛起》

Shanxi merchants endured five centuries of vicissitudes, from the salt trade to the tea business, then reaching a pinnacle with the emergence of exchange firms. They forged a winding 5,150-kilometer Tea Road across the Eurasian continent through their wisdom, tenacity, and strategic acumen, building a grand economic corridor that "connected the world".

The broader the vision, the greater the ambition.

The wealth left by these Shanxi merchants to posterity goes beyond mere luxury mansions. Their legendary stories of exploring the unknown world across thousands of miles resonate throughout history.

第二章　建造辉煌的商业王国

The Magnificent Commercial Empire

Part 2

晋商从脚踏实地、寸积铢累的创业时期，到构建跨国茶叶贸易产业链的成长时期，再到形成多业并举、多元发展产业体系的鼎盛时期，在这张"从无到有"的商业版图上，山西商人成功地建起了一座辉煌的商业王国。

From the down-to-earth and accumulation of resources during the entrepreneurial period, to the growth period of building a cross-border tea trade industry chain, and then to the peak period of forming a multi industry and diversified development industry system, Shanxi merchants have successfully built a brilliant commercial kingdom on this "from scratch" commercial map.

"当时钟敲响四下，世间一切为茶而停下"。这是一首传唱了数百年的英国民谣。生活，被溶进了一杯茶，那一刻，唯有片片茶叶，陪伴时针起舞。

下午茶，是英国人优雅诗意生活的仪式感，更是他们生活的刚需，甚至连打招呼都要问一句："今天你'喝'了吗？"

然而，"宁可一日无食，不可一日无茶"的英国，历史上却不曾种过一片茶叶。茶，被他们称为"神奇的东方树叶"。而让这片东方树叶漂洋过海来到欧洲的，是一群同样蒙着神秘面纱的山西商人，在他们的土地上，也并没有产出过一片茶叶。

中国最早的海外茶叶贸易，为何会发端于不产茶的山西？在车马很慢、书信很远的从前，山西商人是如何打破大半个地球的信息差，解开这一片茶叶的财富密码的呢？

中国首任驻外公使郭嵩焘给出的答案是："山陕商人智术不能望江浙，推算不能及江西湖广，而世守商贾之业，唯其心朴而心实也。"

朴实，是山西人最鲜明的品格，也造就了晋商务实笃行的经营之道。

When the clock struck four, everything in the world stopped for tea. This English folk ballad, passed down for centuries, encapsulates life within a teacup. In that fleeting instance, the graceful movement of the hour hand is accompanied solely by the scattered tea leaves.

Afternoon tea stands as a cherished rite in the refined and poetic life of the British people, a fundamental component of their daily routine. So integral is this practice that they greet one another with the question, "Have you had tea yet?"

However, in the history of Britain, where people believe it's better to go a day without food than a day without tea, has never grown tea. Tea was referred to by them as the magical Oriental leaves. Interestingly, the ones who introduced tea leaves to Europe were the Shanxi merchants, even though their native soil bore no tea of its own.

Why did China's cross-border tea trade start in Shanxi, which didn't produce tea at all? In the days when communication was less convenient, how did these Shanxi merchants overcome the information gap across half the globe and unveil the wealth concealed within the tea leaves?

Guo Songtao, China's first envoy to a foreign country, provided an insight, "Shanxi merchants may lack the sophistication of their counterparts from Jiangsu and Zhejiang, and the calculating capabilities of those from Jiangxi and Huguang. Yet their sincerity and practicality stand unrivaled."

Simplicity is the most distinctive trait of the people of Shanxi. It has forged the business philosophy of being practical and steadfast.

蒙古包
Yurt

壹

在内蒙古锡林郭勒盟的乌拉盖草原深处，牧民赛罕阿姨在网上淘到了一套心仪的奶茶杯。随手下单，不出 3 天，杯子就从山西祁县，飞跃 1000 多公里，送进了蒙古包。但在 300 多年前，牧民们却是猴年马月才能盼来一位挑着货担的货郎。

语言不通、地域阻隔，别说是了解用户需求，在地广人稀的草原上，想要找一个蒙古包都很困难。商人们只能是挑起担子，跑断两条腿，寻找蒙古包上门交易，俗称"货郎担"，蒙语"丹门庆"。在这些"货郎担"中，就有山西太谷商人王相卿。

公元 1696 年，清朝康熙帝御驾西征噶尔丹。山西右玉县的杀虎口，是内地通向蒙古大草原的必经之路。王相卿与同乡张杰、史大学，用三条扁担、六只货箱，挑起担子随军，为屯扎在

寻踪
晋商

银元宝
Silver dollar treasure

银锭
Silver ingot

中国蒙古学学会副会长
内蒙古师范大学教授 王来喜

实际上，旅蒙商帮里面有名的有十大帮，包括京帮、鲁商等等，但为什么只有晋商在蒙古地区受到草原牧民的欢迎呢？因为他们的经营很符合当地的模式，而且他们能了解蒙古族牧民民众的急需和所需。

恰克图茶市
Kiakhtu tea market

　　从柴米油盐、针头线脑开始，山西商人把针尖大的小本生意做成了大商贸。"货郎担"变成了车马驼队，王相卿创办的"大盛魁"也成为响当当的"草原第一商号"，极盛时有员工六七千人、骆驼近两万头，号称"集二十二省之奇货"，上至绸缎，下至葱蒜，无不经营。客户也从草原上的一个个蒙古包拓展到新疆、恰克图，甚至俄国的西伯利亚、莫斯科。当年的大盛魁，仅在外蒙地区的周转资金就高达1000万两白银。它的全部资产到底有多少？史料没有准确统计。不过有人这样形容大盛魁的财富：可以用50两重的银元宝从北京一直铺到蒙古国的乌兰巴托。

多大的,这边一结算,那边便把一群羊赶过去,这一户人家的账就付完了。

春天赊出一包盐,秋天赶回两只羊,追求薄利多销的山西商人,再小的业务也秉持买卖公道、服务周到。他们甚至自学医术,给缺医少药的牧民们看病。他们说蒙语、习蒙礼、着蒙服,是用蒙古话问好"sain bai nu",你好,你父母好吗?你的孩子好吗?你的牛羊好吗?让牧民们觉得他们就像自己的亲戚。

当年山西商人为了学习蒙语,自制了一本用汉语来标注发音的"翻译手册"(新刻校正买卖蒙古同文杂字)。小到蔬菜百货,大到玉石皮毛,静默的书页上似乎能听到买卖交易的喧嚣。

新刻校正买卖蒙古同文杂字
New engraving correction for trading Mongolian characters

草原快递
Grassland Express

蒙古的清军搞后勤，同时提供给养。在向牧民采买牛羊、筹集草料的过程中，他们发现千里草原虽然盛产牲畜、皮毛，但吃饭缺锅、穿衣少布。来自中原的锅碗瓢盆、烟茶粮棉、盐铁制品等日用小百货，都是奇缺之物。

于是，这三个精明的山西商人，把目光转向了茫茫大草原。他们结伴走包串户、送货上门。

内蒙古茶叶之路研究会会长　作家　邓九刚

它和我们现在想象的商业买卖完全是不一样的，是记账、以货易货。秋天、冬天把货送到千家万户，到了来年5月，草长莺飞的好季节开始收账，帐篷是敞开的，付账的那些蒙古族老乡赶着他们的羊群等着货郎算账。丝绸合多少只羊、合几匹马，羊是几个牙的、

大盛魁
Grand and prestigious

　　善于紧盯需求侧动脑筋的山西商人，在和俄罗斯、蒙古商人做生意的过程中发现，这些以肉食为主的民族需要用喝茶来化解油腻，而俄罗斯人尤其对中国的红茶情有独钟。于是，大盛魁自设茶庄，把经营重点转向了茶叶贸易。一眼万里，山西商人的目光，从祖辈创业的支点，远眺向一片比草原更辽阔的商业蓝海。

1 /

On the expansive Ulgai Grassland in Inner Mongolia's Xilingol League, Saihan, who is a herder, bought a set of milk tea cups online. With a mere click, she placed an order, and within three days, the cups from Qixian County in Shanxi Province traveled over 1,000km and was sent into Saihan's yurt.

However, more than three centuries ago, herders could only encounter traveling peddlers once in a blue moon.

With language barriers, and geographical distance, it was difficult to find a yurt on the vast and sparsely populated grasslands, not to mention understanding customer preferences. Traders had no choice but to carry goods with shoulder pole, traverse great distances on foot, look for yurts and trade with herders. Among these traveling peddlers was Wang Xiangqing, a merchant from Taigu, Shanxi.

In 1696, Emperor Kangxi, the fourth emperor of the Qing Dynasty, embarked on a western expedition against Galdan Boshugtu Khan. The Shahu Pass in Youyu County, Shanxi, served as a vital passage to the Mongolian grasslands from the inland regions. Wang Xiangqing, along with his fellow townsmen Zhang Jie and Shi Daxue, carried six crates with three shoulder poles as they followed the army, providing logistical support and provisions for the Qing troops stationed in Mongolia. While buying livestock from herders and gathering fodder, they stumbled upon a fact that despite the large quantities of livestock and furs on the vast grasslands, there was an acute scarcity of essential commodities like cooking utensils and cloth. Ordinary essentials of daily life from the Central Plains like pots, bowls, tobacco, tea, grain, cotton, salt, and iron products were all in high demand.

So, these three perceptive Shanxi merchants shifted their focus toward the expansive grasslands. They visited one yurt after another, delivering goods to the herders' doorsteps.

> **DENG JIUGANG, WRITER**
> **PRESIDENT OF INNER MONGOLIA TEA ROAD**
> **RESEARCH ASSOCIATION**
> They operated differently from what we imagine. They sold goods on credit and bartered with the herders. In winter and autumn, they would deliver goods to countless households. In the following spring, for example, in May, it was time to settle accounts. The yurts would be open, and the local Mongols would bring their sheep and pay their dues. They recorded in detail about how much silk was exchanged for how many sheep or horses, how old the sheep should be, and the size of the sheep. With a single call from the owner, the sheep would come over to the merchants. Then the household's account would be settled.

In spring, a bag of salt was extended on credit, and in autumn, two sheep were returned in payment. Shanxi merchants, who pursued modest profits through high turnover, upheld principles of fairness and attentive service in even the smallest transactions. They even taught themselves medicine to provide healthcare to herders lacking medical care. They spoke the Mongolian language, adhered to Mongolian customs and wore Mongolian clothes. When they delivered goods to their customers, they would greet their customers in the Mongolian language. They would say, "Hello, how are you?How are your parents?How are your children?How are your sheep?How are your horses?"Such a merchant was rather their relative than a businessman.

This is a "translation manual" used by the Shanxi merchants, in which the pronunciations of the Mongolian words were annotated through Chinese characters. The manual includes all kinds of words from vegetables to jade and furs. Through the silent pages of this book, one can almost hear the vibrant echoes of the trade.

Starting with petty commodities, Shanxi merchants transformed their small-scale ventures into big businesses. The travelling peddlers evolved into caravans of wagons and camels. The Dashengkui firm established by Wang Xiangqing became a renowned commercial giant on the grasslands. In its heyday, it employed around 7, 000 people and had more than 20, 000 camels. It sold a wide range of commodities from silk to scallions and garlic. Their clients went from those on the Mongolian grasslands, to those in Xinjiang, Kyakhta, and even Siberia and Moscow in Russia. Back then, Dashengkui had a working capital of 10 million taels of silver in Outer Mongolia alone. The exact total assets remain undocumented, but some people portrayed the wealth of Dashengkui like this. If its wealth was converted into 50-tael silver ingots and the ingots were connected, they would stretch an unbroken path from Beijing all the way to Ulaanbaatar in Mongolia.

WANG LAIXI
VICE PRESIDENT OF CHINA SOCIETY OF MONGOLIA STUDIES
PROFESSOR AT INNER MONGOLIA NORMAL UNIVERSITY

In fact, there were ten well-known groups of merchants in Mongolia, including those from Beijing and Shandong. Why were the Shanxi merchants particularly favored by the local herders? Their business practices were truly in line with the local customs, and they understood the urgent and essential needs of the Mongolian herders.

The savvy Shanxi merchants, who always followed the demand side of the market, realized while doing business with Russian and Mongolian traders that these ethnic groups who have a diet heavy in meat needed tea to counterbalance the grease. Russians had a strong preference for Chinese black tea. Thus, Dashengkui established its own tea house, shifting their focus towards tea trade.

Casting their sights across vast distances, the Shanxi merchants looked beyond the grasslands and shifted their focus from the groundwork established by their ancestors toward an even grander commercial panorama.

贰

武夷山的春夏，为茶而生，也为茶而忙。每到茶期，就有"西客"远道而来。"西客"，山西的"西"，本是当地人对山西商人的一种称呼，后来渐渐演变成了"稀客"，珍稀的"稀"，尊贵的客人。

当时，成群结队的山西商人来到武夷山采购茶叶，沉甸甸的银子被留下，茶叶则从下梅村登船，乘着竹筏西进北上，走过急流险滩，走过戈壁荒原，飘着中国香味的茶，最终被送到欧洲人的餐桌。

数百年来，好奇心驱使着人们去探索这条纵贯南北、联通东西、绵亘万里的茶叶之路。"自古岭北不植茶"，山西是个不种

茶园　Tea plantation

下梅村
Ximay Village

茶的内陆省份。在那个信息闭塞的年代,山西商人是如何把货源地精准定位到隔着千山万水的武夷山,并选择下梅村为起点呢?

龙团凤饼
Dragon group phoenix cake

福建省武夷山下梅村茶商邹氏第29代传人
万里茶道文化产业研究中心顾问　邹全荣

武夷山自古出好茶,比如宋代的龙团凤饼就成为贡茶,进贡给了朝廷。所以在晋商的眼里,必须要花巨大的资金南下武夷山,才能采购到好的茶叶。而且,山西商人的商业嗅觉比较灵敏,那个时候中国茶叶大部分集中在广州这个港口,但因为海禁的原因,茶叶没有办法海运,南茶北销,这是最好时机。

万里茶道起点
The starting point of the tea ceremony

  历经明清两代，数百年口外经商的山西商人，不仅积累了大量财富，也把审时度势的商业基因根植到血脉中。他们一边打听着武夷山销路不畅、茶园过剩、茶价低迷的消息，一边紧盯俄罗斯和蒙古草原茶叶需求增长、价格飙升的市场走势。他们甚至把商业触角延伸到9000公里外的英吉利海峡。

  在那里，有一位超级爱喝茶的葡萄牙公主，她嫁给了英国国王查理二世，也把饮茶文化传入了英国。从皇家贵族到城市平民，家家户户的作息表上，从此多了一段雷打不动的"下午茶时间"。

寻踪
晋商

茶叶走入欧洲人日常生活
Tea entered everyday life in Europe

大益集团法国籍国际交流专员　孙博

在17、18世纪，茶确实多见于欧洲的上流社会。18世纪之后，在公元1722年，英国56%的进口产品都是茶。茶叶的进口额，在18世纪中叶，有1200万英镑，是一个巨大的数字。

一贯审时度势、务实经营的山西商人，此时，又笃定地做出一个极具前瞻性的战略选择。公元1755年，山西商人常万达远赴武夷山购买茶山，由此种出了一片枝繁叶茂的产业森林。

福建省武夷山下梅村茶商邹氏第29代传人　邹全荣

下梅村的后山上，曾经都是原始植被，甚至是荒凉的，山西商人看

> 中了这些资源，就把这里开辟成茶园，和当地的茶商进行了资本的融合、技术的融合和贸易资源的整合。茶厂、街市上的一些店铺，包括老字号的包装经营，都是一条龙式的。

一边购买茶山种茶，一边设庄收购扩大货源，小村庄发展为大茶市。为了让竹筏、茶船深入到街区，穿村而过的过水沟也被开凿成了人工小运河，长度仅有900米的当溪，就拥有着9个埠位。每逢收获季，采摘下来的散茶被加工成发酵茶，再经过水运、陆运和驼运，抵达恰克图买卖城，再卖到俄国腹地和其他欧洲国家。

中国有句俗话："开门七件事，柴米油盐酱醋茶。"而当年的山西商人，愣是把排在末尾的茶，做成了一种硬通货。当时，俄罗斯和蒙古地区的人们尤其偏爱山西人销售的砖茶，甚至把它当作货币使用。

俄国蒙古学学者阿·马·波兹德涅耶夫在他的日记《蒙古及蒙古人》中有这样一段记述："库伦一间客房连饭费一昼夜付一块砖茶，合60—65银戈比""一普特干草卖到两块砖茶""木材商每年出售木材价值三百到六百箱砖茶"。近200年过去了，这些地方的人们对砖茶的情有独钟，依然未减分毫，买茶时一定要先看一看上面那个"川"字。

内蒙古草原茶路协会会长　孛·乌兰娜
> 好多牧民因为不会说汉语，看到砖茶的时候，首先要找三道杠"川"字，牧民把"川"字牌茶叶称作"鸟爪子茶"。

"川"字牌茶
"Chuan" brand tea

蒙古国中国历史文化研究协会会长　巴特尔夫
当时汉口有许多茶叶加工厂，有三个大的工厂，其中之一专门生产向蒙古销售的"川"字牌茶叶。"川"字牌砖茶对蒙古人民的生活产生了较大影响，直到今天，一些寺庙的建筑上，还能看到"川"字形图案。

"川"字是怎么来的呢？有两种说法：一个说法是来自山西商人渠同海，渠同海在自己家族里排行川字辈；另一个说法是羊楼洞这个地方有三条泉水——石人泉、观音泉、凉荫泉。喝茶的人都知道，好山好水出好茶，好水是制茶的关键之一。在一块清代时期由晋商出资修葺的观音泉纪念石碑上，刻着众多晋商商号，比如长盛川、长裕川、大昌川、大玉川，这就是"两大两长"。公元1861年，几位山西商人一起决定，把羊楼洞生产的砖茶统一为"川"字标，并由"两大两长"四家最富盛名的茶庄做监制。

山西财经大学工商管理学院院长　卫虎林

"川"字标背后反映的就是当时晋商强烈的品质意识，或者叫品牌意识。品牌最本质、最核心的就是消费者对它的认知、信任，"川"字牌的背后，是四大商业翘楚对"川"字牌的监督。监督什么？就是监督它的品质。

其实，这个被印在茶砖上的"川"字，早在100多年前，就被刻在了

祁县渠家门楣
Qi county canal family lintel

晋商大贾祁县渠家的门楣上。"纳川"二字，代表"聚拢财富"，更寓意"海纳百川"。

方寸之心，可纳百川。门楣上的一笔一画，雕刻风骨、雕镂人心。正是这样的风骨，铸就了一条越走越远的"万里茶道"。

山西大学晋商学研究所副所长　刘成虎

从空间上而言，万里茶道可以粗略地分为四大功能区：第一是湖闽茶产地，是非常重要的茶叶生产加工制作基地；第二是中北地区的茶贸区，它是货物仓储集散的物流中心、物流基地；第三是俄蒙茶市的交易中心、交易基地。而我们晋商故里则是茶叶交易非常重要的商务指挥中心，这是一条非常完整的产业链。产业链的配套率，完整度越高，竞争力就越强。从我们今天这个角度来看，早在260多年前，晋商已经拥有了这种产业链发展的思维和高质量发展的理念，并且付诸经营实践之中。

那些留在青砖上的车辙印痕，见证着当年万里茶道商务指挥中心的车水马龙。从这里起笔，19世纪的中国，在世界商业版图上率先画出一条完整的茶产业链。而山西商帮也完成了从商业资本向产业资本的精彩一跃，并由此开启了他们在中国贸易史上的全盛时期。

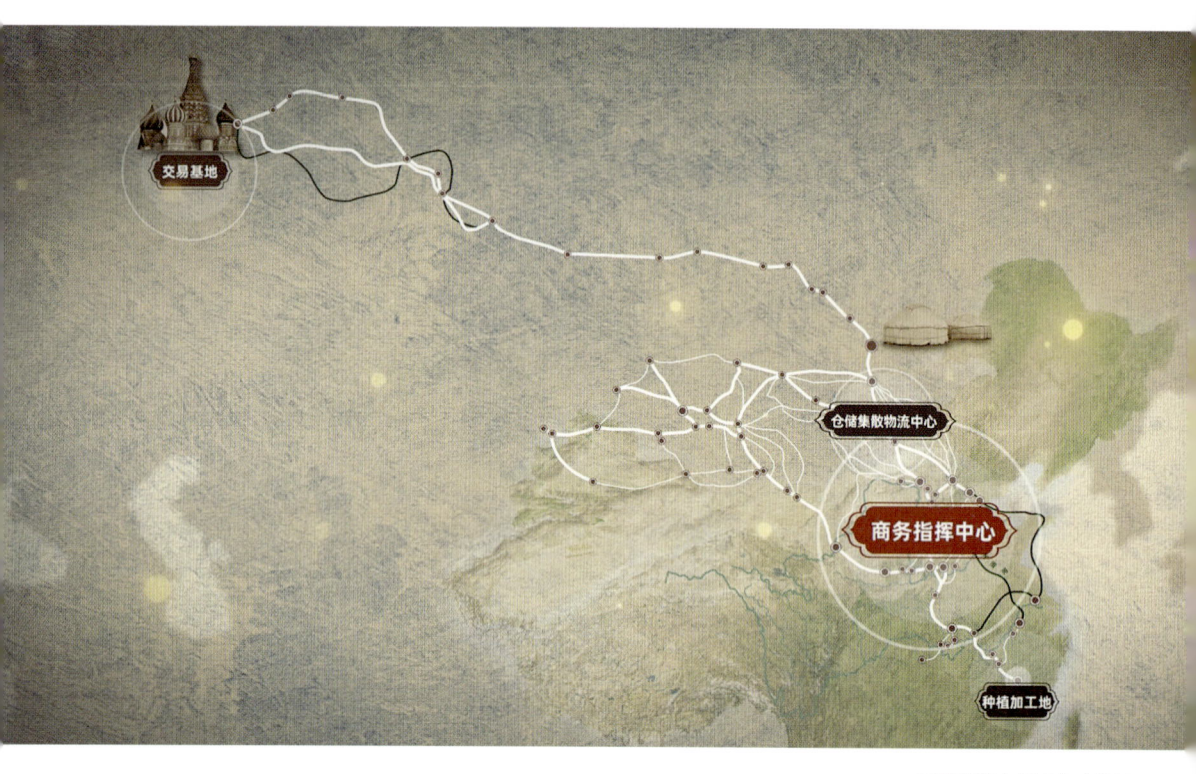

万里茶道上的四大功能区
Four functional areas on the tea ceremony

寻踪晋商

2

In the Wuyi Mountain, spring and summer are seasons about tea. At this time of a year, Xike, meaning guests from Shanxi, would come. The local people referred to Shanxi merchants as Xike. Later, the word evolved and got the meaning of rare and distinguished guests.

Shanxi merchants came here to purchase tea leaves. Hefty sums of silver were left behind, while the tea leaves embarked on a journey from Xiamei Village to Europe. They sailed downriver on bamboo rafts, traversed swift currents, crossed desolate deserts, and went all the way to the dining tables of the European people.

For centuries, curiosity drove people to explore the tea road stretching for thousands of miles. It stretches from north to south and connects east and west. Tea doesn't grow north of the Qinling Mountains since ancient times. Shanxi is a landlocked province that doesn't produce tea. In an era of limited information exchange, how did the Shanxi merchants precisely locate the source of goods in the distant Wuyi Mountain, and why did they choose Xiamei Village as their starting point?

> **ZOU QUANRONG, 29TH-GENERATION DESCENDANT OF TEA MERCHANT FAMILY OF ZOU OF XIAMEI VILLAGE**
>
> Wuyi Mountain has been renowned for its fine teas since ancient times. For example, the Song Dynasty's Dragon and Phoenix Tea Cake was offered to the imperial court as a tribute. In the eyes of the Shanxi merchants, purchasing tea from Wuyi Mountain required substantial financial investment. Moreover, Shanxi merchants possessed a keen business acumen. During that time,

the majority of China's tea was concentrated in the port of Guangzhou. However, due to the ban on maritime trade, tea couldn't be transported via waterways. This was the best opportunity to sell the tea from the south to the north.

In the Ming and Qing Dynasties, Shanxi merchants, who'd been engaged in foreign trade for centuries, achieved substantial riches. The ability of size up the situation was deeply rooted in their genes. In this pivotal era, they adeptly gathered information about the sluggish sales of tea leaves from the Wuyi Mountain, the glut of tea leaves, and the low prices of tea leaves. Meanwhile, they kept an eye on the market in Russia and Mongolian grasslands, where the demand for tea leaves was surging where the demand for tea leaves was surging and tea prices escalating. Their commercial activities also expanded to the English Channel 9,000km away.

In that distant land resided a Portuguese princess with an ardent affection for tea who married King Charles II of England. She introduced tea drinking to England. Influenced by her, having afternoon tea became a new daily routine for all those in England, from the royal family to the ordinary people.

JULIEN BONZON,
FRENCH INTERNATIONAL EXCHANGE SPECIALIST,
TAETEA GROUP

During the 17th and 18th centuries, tea was exclusive to the elite circles in Europe. In the 18th century, precisely in 1722, tea claimed a remarkable 56% share among the goods imported to Britain. The imports of tea surged to a staggering 12 million pounds in the mid-18th century.

Pragmatic and forward-thinking, the Shanxi merchants made yet another resolute and visionary strategic decision. In 1755, Shanxi merchant Chang Wanda journeyed far to Wuyi Mountain to acquire hills to build tea gardens, marking the birth of a prosperous tea cultivation enterprise. As you can see, there are some hills behind the village. In the past, these hills were covered in primal vegetation, and some were even desolate. Seeing the value of these resources, Shanxi merchants transformed them into tea gardens. They cooperated with local tea merchants in terms of capital, technology and trade resources. They were engaged in all processes of the industrial chain, from the operation of tea factories and shops, to the packaging of tea leaves.

While buying hills to build tea gardens and setting up shops to amplify their inventory, a small village swiftly transformed into a bustling tea market. To enable bamboo rafts and ships to go into the village, the waterways meandering through the village were converted into canals. The unassuming Dangxi Creek, spanning a modest 900 meters, proudly harbored nine berths.

In the harvest season, the plucked tea leaves underwent a transformation into fermented tea. Then, the tea was transported by boat, by land and by camels to Kyakhta and the Buy-and-Sell City, before eventually finding their way to the heart of Russia and other European countries.

> **BO ULANA, PRESIDENT**
> **GRASSLAND TEA ROAD ASSOCIATION OF INNER MONGOLIA**
> Many herders couldn't speak the Chinese language. When they bought tea bricks, they would look for the character Chuan first. They called this brand birds' claw or three vertical lines.

> **KHORLOO BAATARKHUU, CHAIRMAN**
> **MONGOLIAN ASSOCIATION FOR CHINESE HISTORY**
> **AND CULTURE**
>
> Back then, there were lots of tea factories in Hankou. Three of them were large, one of which specialized in the production of tea bricks of the Chuan brand. It was owned by Shanxi merchants and sold to Mongolia. This kind of tea bricks has had huge influence on the life of the Monglos. Even today, we can still see the patterns of Chuan on some temple buildings.

The origin of the character of Chuan has two mainstream explanations. One theory is that a prominent Shanxi merchant was named Qu Tonghai. The family members of his generation all had the character Chuan in their names. Another explanation pertains to Yangloudong, where there are three springs, namely Shiren Spring, Guanyin Spring, and Liangyin Spring. The Guanyin Spring we are currently standing by is represented by the central vertical line of the character. As tea enthusiasts know, good tea often comes from areas with good mountains and water. Quality water is one of the crucial factors in tea production. This stone monument, dating back to the Qing Dynasty, stands as a tribute to the benevolence of Shanxi merchants who joined hands with the inhabitants of Yangloudong to restore the Guanyin Spring. Names of a lot of firms set up by Shanxi merchants are inscribed on it, such as Changyuchuan, Changshengchuan, Dachangchuan, and Dayuchuan.

In 1861, several Shanxi merchants decided that all the tea bricks produced in Yangloudong should be marketed under the brand of Chuan. The task of supervising the production was given to the four most distinguished tea factories.

> **WEI HULIN, DEAN**
> **FACULTY OF BUSINESS ADMINISTRATION, SHANXI**
> **UNIVERSITY OF FINANCE AND ECONOMICS**
> Behind this lies the strong emphasis on quality or brand awareness that the Shanxi merchants possessed during that time. For a brand, the most essential thing was consumers' recognition and trust. Behind the brand of Chuan was the supervision from the four leading tea factories. What did they focus on? It was quality.

In fact, over 100 years ago, the character of Chuan imprinted on the tea brick was already carved on the lintel of the prominent Qu family in Qixian County, Shanxi. The word Nachuan symbolizes the accumulation of wealth, which carries the deeper meaning of "being tolerant to diversity".

A humble heart has the capacity to embrace immense diversity. Every stroke and curve carved on the lintel embodies the character and spirit of the local people. It is this very character and spirit that gave rise to the long Tea Road.

> **LIU CHENGHU**
> **DEPUTY DIRECTOR, INSTITUTE OF SHANXI**
> **MERCHANTS STUDIES, SHANXI UNIVERSITY**
> The Tea Road could be roughly divided into four main functional areas. The tea factories in Hubei and Fujian served as the planting and processing base, Zhongbei Tea Trade was the warehousing, distribution and logistics base, the tea market in Russia and Mongolia functioned as the trading base, and the homeland of Shanxi merchants acted as the business headquarters. These four areas essentially formed what we now refer to as an industrial chain. The

higher the match rate of the industrial chain was, the stronger the industrial competitiveness it had. Seen from today, Shanxi merchants already had this kind of industrial chain mindset and high-quality development concept, and they also put them into practice over 260 years ago.

The wheel tracks left on these green bricks bear witness to the bustling scenes of the business headquarters along the Tea Road. Starting from here, the 19th-century China pioneered a complete tea industry chain on the world's business map. Shanxi merchants also accomplished a remarkable transformation from commercial capital to industrial capital, thus ushering in their most glorious period in China's trade history.

湖北武汉
Wuhan, Hubei

叁

　　武汉的早晨，从一碗热干面开始。热干面＋豆皮、热干面＋油条、热干面＋油饼烧麦……流水的"过早"餐，铁打的热干面，它的江湖地位数百年来未曾动摇。武汉人"过早"的传统来自长江码头。一夜的辛苦劳作后，低价、饱腹、高热量的"碳水炸弹"，是码头工人和天南地北的生意人最佳的能量源。

　　武汉素有"东方茶港"之称，因为这里曾是万里茶道上最大的集散地。19世纪中叶，中国对俄茶叶出口量剧增，但跨国贸易意味着更遥远的距离、更强大的运力和更先进的保鲜方式。今天，有了多式联运、中欧班列，一箱二三十吨的茶叶运往俄罗斯，10多天就能到达。而当年茶货从武汉中转上船，再船倒车、车转

武汉阳逻新港
Wuhan Yangluo New Port

驼，辗转数月才能运抵中俄边境。

《山西外贸志》中记载："当格兰顿将军周游世界来到俄罗斯，万万没想到，到处都是山西商人。"一业兴，百业旺，一片漂洋过海的茶叶，还能打开多少未知的产业空间？

甘肃政法大学丝路法学院俄罗斯籍教授　奥莉娅
除了茶叶，我们看到还有毛皮、谷物和其它商品的交易，这些都是相互关联的。

湖北大学历史文化学院院长
日本山口大学东亚研究所客座教授　黄柏权

北上的主要是以茶叶为主，南方的丝绸布匹、中原的粮食运到恰克图以后，驼队必须要计算成本，所以又从俄罗斯、西伯利亚等地买来毛皮和欧洲的工业品，来回都有货物，加强了贸易往来，从而实现利润的最大化。

粮米药材之路、皮毛骡马之路、食盐布帛百货之路……辅线、支线众多的万里茶道引发了深刻的产业连带效应，茶产区的种植业与加工业、沿途的水陆运输业、沿线城市的各商业品类、西伯利亚的工业都因之繁荣。与古代丝绸之路、茶马古道，以及后来的海上丝绸之路等，共同构成了世界文明史上东西方经济文化交流的重要通道。

湖北大学历史文化学院院长
日本山口大学东亚研究所客座教授　黄柏权

万里茶道兴起的时期，正好是丝绸之路衰落的时期。从空间上，它们有重叠；从时间上，它们有接替；从贸易运输来看，它接替了原来东西向丝绸之路所有的商贸功能。因为万里茶道从茶源地到消费地，整个运输线路呈网状式分布。各类信息、资金、文化沿着这样一个网络很好地流动起来，流动到国外，加入了国际大市场，把中国经济纳入了世界贸易体系中，促进了中国加入世界全球化、一体化的进程。

呼和浩特塞上老街
Hohhot Sai Shang Old Street

  人流、物流、资金流、信息流，川流不息，牵动着沿线7省29个城市，甚至欧亚大陆。这条跨越欧亚的"世纪动脉"，如同一台不停运转的机器；它的产品，是不断生长出的千行百业。

  在今天有一个家喻户晓的词，叫"物流"。"一骑红尘妃子笑，无人知是荔枝来。"这句描述把南方的鲜荔枝运到北方的诗句，可以说是中国古代物流行业的著名案例。而山西商人的跨国贸易，要从四季如春的南方跨越到冰天雪地的北方，单靠马力显然是不够的，是骆驼成就了那个时代的"海淘"。

  内蒙古呼和浩特，也就是当年的归化城，是商贸往来的必经之地。众多养骆驼、拉骆驼的人汇聚于此，使这里成为名副其实的"骆驼村"。

张库大道局部地貌
Zhangku Avenue local landform

万里茶道鼎盛时期，这里养着 20 万峰骆驼。当年"骆驼村"的驼户中，山西人是中坚力量。他们有的靠拉骆驼白手起家，置办起商铺；有的凭着无远不往、无深不至的韧劲，从一介驼夫发展到组建驼队，成为与茶商比肩的大驼商。

沿着今天的呼和浩特麻花板村、厂汉板村、五路村一路走来，仍能看到许多山西籍后代。

当年的漫漫茶路，没有公、铁、水、空的交通网络，山西商人就发明了那个时代的"多式联运"。一双脚、几峰驼，脚夫搬、车马运、水转陆、陆转驼，以骆驼村为支点，以家乡山西和邻省河北为物流中枢，山西商人撬动了"南来烟酒糖布茶，北来骆驼牛羊马"的跨国物流贸易。

然而，万里茶道，漫漫征途。山西商人的车马驼队，载着越驮越重的金银，也载着未知的机遇和不测的风险。

呼和浩特五路村村民　山西右玉驼户后代　石茂

拉骆驼是最苦的营生，春天走了，有时候到了秋天，甚至冬天才能回来。

呼和浩特麻花板村村民　山西五台驼户后代　董文

路上会遇上一群一群的狼，特别危险，着急了就让土匪劫了。

自古商道是险道，土匪强盗，七灾八难。面对这个生死攸关的难题，能不能找到一个务实的破题之道？

中国古代有一个十分神秘的职业，在影视作品和武侠小说中，他们个个武功高强，而且一诺千金、心怀大义。这个职业就是镖师，它的鼻祖就是张黑五。张黑五曾是乾隆皇帝的武术老师，

晋剧《日昇昌记》剧照
Jin opera "Risheng Chang Ji" stills

镖局

Escort service

这位武功盖世的山西汉子因为脸黑，在兄弟中排行老五，所以人称"神拳无敌"张黑五。

层出不穷的武林高手，被高价聘请押运现银和重要货物，中国最早的保险押运业就在万里茶道上诞生了。因势而起、乘势而兴的镖局，从此成为山西商人产业体系中的重要组成部分。

山西省晋商文化研究会常务理事　张宪平

晋商的务实经营，体现在他们的行动力上。晋商去开拓万里茶道，一开始他们是去收购成品茶，搞长途贩运。围绕长途贩运，他们又延伸出了物流、保险押运这些新业态。到后来他们就自己买茶山、种茶树、制茶叶、创造品牌，从商品的流通领域进入到商品的生产领域。晋商之所以能够步步走在前头，是因为他们能够在各个历史

镖箱
Dart case

太谷志一堂镖箱
Taitani Chi a dart box

晋商产业图
Jinshang industry map

时期发现"机遇窗口",发现各个地区的潜力和优势,而且能马上付诸行动,一步一步去落实。晋商全方位的成功,和他们的务实笃行的人格素质是密切相关的。

从脚踏实地、寸积铢累的创业时代,到抓住"窗口期"构建跨国产业链的成长时代,再到在商言商,形成多业并举、多元发展产业体系的鼎盛时代。这张"从无到有"的商业版图上,山西商人的商业脉络越来越清晰。

3 /

Morning in Wuhan start with a bowl of hot-dry noodles. Such noodles can be paired with tofu skin, deep-fried dough sticks, deep-fried dough cakes, and Shaomai. Despite the ever-changing breakfast, the position of hot-dry noodles in the culinary world has remained unwavering for centuries. The breakfast tradition in Wuhan originates from the Yangtze River docks. After a night of hard work, the low-cost, filling, high-calorie and high-carbohydrate food became the ideal source of energy for dock workers and businessmen from all over the country.

Wuhan is known as the Eastern Tea Port due to its history as a major distribution center along the ancient Tea Road. In the mid-19th century, China's export of tea to Russia surged. However, international trade meant longer distances, greater transportation capabilities, and advanced preservation methods. Today, with multimodal transportation and the China-Europe Railway Express, a shipment of 20 or 30 tons of goods can be sent to Russia in about 10 days. Yet, in the past, tea was loaded onto ships in Wuhan, and then transferred by wagons and camels. It took several months to transport tea from Wuhan to the border of China and Russia.

As recorded in the Foreign Trade Annals of Shanxi, when General Ulysess S. Grant traveled to Russia, he was surprised to find Shanxi merchants everywhere. The thriving of one industry boosted the development of numerous other industries. How much untapped potential could tea leaves from the other side of the ocean unleash?

Except for tea, there was also the trade of fur, cereals, and other goods. They were all interrelated. The commodities sent to the north were mainly tea leaves. Silk and cloth from the south and grains from the Central

Plains were transported to Kyakhta. Cost counting was essential for camel caravans. Then they purchased furs from Siberia in Russia. Later, industrial products were purchased from Europe. With goods transported from both sides, they maximized their profits.

The myriad auxiliary and branch routes of the Tea Road, such as the Grain and Medicine Route, the Fur and Livestock Route, the Salt, Cloth, and General Merchandise Route, led to profound industrial ripple effects. The tea planting and processing sectors in tea-producing regions, along with the land and water transport along the routes, the diverse sectors in cities along the routes, and the industry in Siberia, all thrived. The Tea Road, the ancient Silk Road, the Tea Horse Road, and the Maritime Silk Road served as important conduits for economic and cultural interactions between the East and the West.

> **HUANG BAIQUAN,**
> **DEAN OF SCHOOL OF HISTORY AND CULTURE, HUBEI UNIVERSITY**
> **GUEST PROFESSOR AT GRADUATE SCHOOL OF EAST ASIAN STUDIES, YAMAGUCHI UNIVERSITY OF JAPAN**
>
> The rise of the Tea Road coincided with the wane of the Silk Road. Spatially, they overlapped. Temporally, the Tea Road replaced the Silk Road. In terms of trade and transportation, the Tea Road assumed all functions of the former east-west Silk Road. This is because the Tea Road's distribution network, spanning from tea-producing regions to consumption hubs, facilitated the smooth flow of diverse elements such as information, capital, and culture. This network seamlessly brought China's economy into the global trade framework, integrating China into the process of globalization.

The continuous flow of population, commodities, capital, and information boosted the development of 29 cities in 7 provinces along the Tea Road and even the development on the Eurasian continent. This cross-continental artery of the century operated as an unceasing mechanism, giving rise to innumerable thriving sectors.

Today, the term logistics is widely known. As a steed raised red dust the imperial concubine smiled;No one knew it was for the lychees it had brought. This poetic description of transporting fresh lychees from the south to the north was a renowned case in China's ancient logistics industry. However, horsepower was obviously insufficient for the cross-border trade conducted by Shanxi merchants, who traversed from the warm south to the world of ice and snow in Siberia. It was camels, instead of horses, that made overseas shopping possible.

Hohhot in Inner Mongolia, formerly known as Guihua, was an indispensable hub for trade and commerce. It served as a gathering place for camel breeders and camel caravans, earning it the name of the Camel Village.

When the Tea Road was in its heyday, there were 200, 000 camels raised here. The people from Shanxi played a major role among the camel breeders in the Camel Village. Some started from using camels for transport and gradually established their own businesses. Others, driven by an unwavering determination, turned from camel drivers to camel caravan owners who were as prominent as tea traders. In today's Mahuaban Village, Changhanban Village, and Wulu Village in Hohhot, there are still many people of Shanxi origin. Among them is Shi Mao, originally from Youyu County of Shanxi.

Back then, there were no highways, railways, waterways or air routes along the meandering Tea Road. Shanxi merchants invented the multimodal transportation of that era. Relying on foot, camels, wagons and boats, and with the Camel Village serving as a pivot and Shanxi and Hebei as logistics hubs, Shanxi merchants were actively involved in cross-border logistics and managed to transport commodities from southern China to other countries. However, along the vast expanse of the Tea Road, Shanxi merchants' caravans, laden with large amount of gold and silver, also faced unknown opportunities and unforeseen risks.

Throughout history, trade routes have been fraught with peril, plagued by bandits and robbers. Confronted with this life-and-death challenge, could a practical solution be found?

There was a mysterious profession in ancient China, often depicted in martial arts films and novels as Kungfu masters who were faithful to their promises and willing to stand up for justice. This legendary profession, escort master, and he was Zhang Heiwu. He once served as the martial arts instructor to Emperor Qianlong. This man from Shanxi was known as Zhang Heiwu, the Invincible Fist, due to his exceptional martial prowess, his dark complexion, and his status as the fifth son in his family.

Numerous martial arts masters were hired at high prices to escort silver and important goods, giving rise to China's earliest insurance escort industry along the Tea Road. Riding the tide of opportunity, the thriving escort agencies became a crucial component of Shanxi merchants' industrial framework.

> **ZHANG XIANPING, MANAGING DIRECTOR**
> **SHANXI MERCHANTS CULTURE RESEARCH**
> **ASSOCIATION OF SHANXI PROVINCE**
> An important aspect of the pragmatic operation of Jinshang is the ability to act. When the Jin merchants went to develop the Wanli Tea Ceremony, they went to buy finished tea at the beginning and engaged in long-distance trafficking. Around long-distance trafficking, they have extended new business formats

such as logistics, insurance, and escort. Later, they bought tea mountains, planted tea trees, made tea, and created brands, which was to enter the field of commodity production from the field of commodity circulation. The reason why Jin merchants were able to take the lead step by step was that they were not only able to discover the "window of opportunity" in various historical periods, discover the potential and advantages of each region, but also immediately put them into action and implement them step by step. The all-round success of the Jin merchants is closely related to their pragmatic personality quality.

They were down-to-earth and accumulated their wealth little by little in the early days of their businesses. Then they seized the opportunity windows and established cross-border industrial chains. Later, they ushered in the golden age when they were engaged in various industries. The commercial network of Shanxi merchants became increasingly discernible on this ever-evolving canvas of business.

平遥古城一角
Pingyao ancient city corner

肆

今天，遍布全球的金融中心，永远占据着一座城市最高大最耀眼的建筑，似乎这是它们从娘胎里带来的高贵气质。

与他们相比，常常被人们称为中国银行业"乡下外祖父"的日昇昌略显清简朴素。可谁都不会忘记，这位朴实低调的"外祖父"，却有过闪耀历史舞台的传奇人生。它，曾创造了"执中国金融之牛耳"的辉煌功业。

19世纪20年代，随着万里茶道产业体系的不断扩张和跨国贸易的日益繁盛，在茶商分支机构所在地，聪明的山西商人，用一张薄薄的麻纸代替了沉甸甸的实银押运。票号汇兑业务兴起，一种全新的经济业态诞生了。

"蔚"字五联号

"蔚"字五联号
The word "Wei" is five couplets

平遥日昇昌是山西票号的始祖,可即便是在最鼎盛时,日昇昌总部的管理者和工作人员也就十几人,遍布全国的各分号通常也只有三四名员工。43家这样的山西票号,却不动声色地控制着全国80%的资金流向。晋商是如何在短短几年间把中国金融业推向一个新高度的?我们可以从"日昇昌"的竞争对手——毛鸿翙和他所创办的"蔚"字五联号中寻找踪迹。

毛鸿翙与日昇昌的创始人雷履泰,这两位商业奇才本是一对生意上的好拍档,后来因为经营理念不一致,分道扬镳。毛鸿翙被介休富商侯氏高薪聘请,开拓票号业务。侯家虽商铺林立,但资本分散、人才不足,200

多个商号，没有一家能与日昇昌匹敌。侯东家与毛掌柜反复思谋，决定把侯家名下的蔚泰厚、蔚丰厚、蔚盛长、天成亨、新泰厚5个绸布庄一口气都改成票号，联手与日昇昌一决高下，号称"蔚"字五联号。

山西省晋商学与区域经济发展协同中心研究员　荣晓峰

"雷毛之争"实际上也并不是一种你死我活的争斗，从两家票号的建筑风格我们也可以看出，蔚泰厚的房顶甚至比日昇昌还要稍低一点，这恰恰是我们晋商的特质，踏实务本、低调经营。这种特质使得山西票号业从寡头垄断走向了自由竞争，这也是票号业的一种良性竞争。

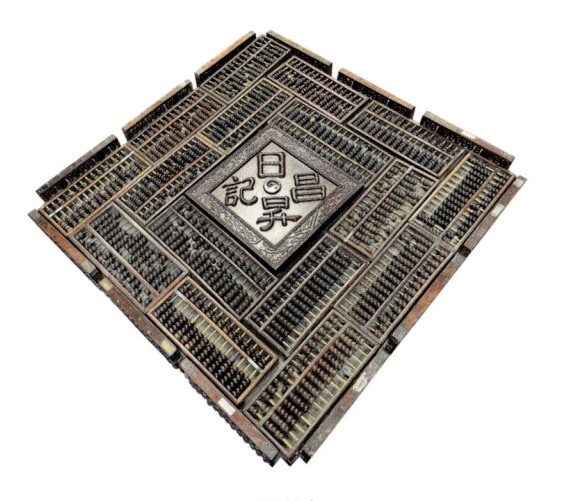

日昇昌算盘
Sunrise and Chang abacus

"蔚"字五联号用"合纵战略"打破了日昇昌的垄断地位，毛鸿翙开创性地推出一种松散型的集团经营模式。平遥总号统辖各地分号的业务范围、经营策略，仲裁各号间的摩擦分歧；分号则自主经营、独立核算，因为全国各地的分号有大有小，为了科学决策、高效管理，各地均由大商号统领小商号。这样的经营模式，极大地提升了企业抗御风险的能力。鼎盛时期，"蔚"字五联号在北京、天津、上海、苏州、杭州、宁波、厦门等50个大中城市广设分号，总号和分号之间资金相互周转，"千里一呼，无不响应"。

> **上海财经大学讲席教授**
> **山西财经大学晋商研究院学术院长　燕红忠**
> 通过总分号和联号制度所形成的商业网点，为山西票号开展汇兑业务提供了直接的硬件基础。当时的一位俄国领事在《长城外的中国西部地区》这本书中说："山西商人具有大商业才能，早在19世纪的中国，就已经形成了现代美国托拉斯式的跨国企业集团的雏形。"

从历史烟尘中走出的山西商人，很快迎来了金融资本的繁荣鼎盛。先后出现在平遥城的22家票号，曾在全国77个城镇设立400多个分号，甚至远到俄罗斯、日本、朝鲜等国家。他们把贸易网、融资网、汇兑网联成一张"汇通天下"的庞大金融网络。金融资本与产业资本深度交融，山西商人成功建起一座辉煌的商业王国。

平遥总号职责图
Pingyao general number responsibility map

分号职责图
Semicolon responsibility chart

Tracing Shanxi Merchants

PART 2

094－095

寻踪
晋商

日昇昌票号旧址
Risheng Chang ticket number old site

日升昌印章　Risheng Chang Sea

4

In the world today, global financial centers always boast tall and dazzling skyscrapers, as if they were born with an inherent air of nobility.

In comparison, this unassuming courtyard is often referred to as the countryside grandfather of China's banking industry. Yet, no one could forget that this humble grandfather had lived a legendary life on the grand stage of history, as someone who once held the reins of Chinese finance.

In the 1920s, as the Tea Road's industrial network continued to expand and cross-border trade flourished, the wise Shanxi merchants, based in the places where tea business branches were located, replaced heavy silver ingots with thin sheets of hemp paper. The rise of Piaohao, or private banks, marked the birth of an entirely new economic form.

Rishengchang of Pingyao was the first private bank established by Shanxi merchants. Even in its heyday, its headquarters had a mere handful of managers and workers. Each of its branches also had a modest staff of three or four. Yet, 43 such private banks set up by Shanxi merchants controlled 80% of the nation's capital flow.

How did the Shanxi merchants push China's financial industry to new heights in just a few years? We can find some clues from Mao Honghui, the rival of Rishengchang, and his Yu Associates.

Mao Honghui and Lei Lvtai, the founder of Rishengchang, were originally business partners. However, due to their different business philosophies, they eventually went their separate ways. Mao Honghui was hired at a high salary by the wealthy Hou family in Jiexiu to develop private banking business.

While possessing an array of stores, the Hou family faced problems of thinly spread capital and lack of talents. None of its 200 stores could measure up to the stature of Rishengchang. After deliberate consideration, Mao Honghui and the owner of the stores decided to change their five silk stores, namely Yutaihou, Yufenghou, Yushengchang, Tianchengheng, Xintaihou, into private banks collectively known as the Yu Associates to compete with Rishengchang.

> **RONG XIAOFENG, RESEARCH FELLOW**
> **SHANXI MERCHANT STUDIES AND REGIONAL ECONOMIC COORDINATION AND DEVELOPMENT CENTER OF SHANXI PROVINCE**
>
> The Lei-Mao rivalry wasn't a life-or-death struggle. In fact, when observing the buildings of the two private banks, we can find that the roof of the building of Yutaihou was even slightly lower than that of Rishengchang. This precisely reflects the characteristic of Shanxi merchants, pragmatic, down-to-earth, and modest. Because of these traits, Shanxi merchants' private banking business went from monopoly to free competition. The competition in the industry was healthy.

The Yu Associates broke the monopoly held by Rishengchang. Mao Honghui invented the loose conglomerate business model. The headquarters in Pingyao managed the scope of operations and business strategies for various branch offices, and arbitrated the conflicts between them. Each branch office operated independently with separate accounting. Given the varying sizes of the branches, larger ones oversaw smaller ones to make decision-making more scientific and management efficient. This operational approach significantly bolstered the Associates' ability to withstand risks.

During its peak, the Associates had branches in 50 major cities, including Beijing,

Tianjin, Shanghai, Suzhou, Hangzhou, Ningbo, and Xiamen. Funds flowed smoothly between the headquarters and the branch offices.

> YAN HONGZHONG
> CHAIR PROFESSOR AT SHANGHAI UNIVERSITY OF FINANCE
> AND ECONOMICS
> ACADEMIC DEAN OF INSTITUTE OF SHANXI MERCHANT
> STUDIES, SHANXI UNIVERSITY OF FINANCE AND ECONOMICS
> The network formed by the headquarters and branch offices provided a solid foundation for Shanxi's private banking business. In his book China's Western Regions Beyond the Great Wall, a Russian consul noted that Shanxi merchants possessed great business acumen, and in the 19th century in China, they already laid the foundation for the multinational corporations like Trust in modern America.

Shanxi merchants soon witnessed the rise of financial capital. A total of 22 private banks were established in Pingyao, with over 400 branch offices in 77 towns nationwide. They even had branches in Russia, Japan, and Korea. They connected the networks of trade, finance and exchange into a colossal financial web that connected the world. With deeply intertwined financial capital and industrial capital, Shanxi merchants managed to build a magnificent commercial empire.

一片春茶绿，掀动产业浪潮风起云涌；阵阵驼铃响，载出"世纪动脉"贯通中外；滚滚算珠跃，开创金融先河引领全国。

端起历史的望远镜，回望传奇商帮建造的这座辉煌商业王国，就会发现，这个传奇商帮的足印，深深地镌刻在了人类商业文明的探索之路上。

那是寸积铢累、以末致富的商业奇迹；那是脚踏实地、求真务实的民族基因；那是审时度势、在商言商的中国智慧。

数百年间，他们热闹过，也沉寂过；他们走进历史，又走出历史，但却从未走远！他们幻化成时间罗盘上的记忆，深入到社会机体的血脉，变成无处不在的存在。

纪录片《寻踪晋商》第二集：
《建造辉煌的商业王国》

With green tea leaves, they set off a wave of industrial transformation.

In the jingle of camel bells, they paved the way for the artery of the century connecting China and the rest of the world.

As abacus beads bounced, they brazed a new trail in the financial industry.

As we cast our gaze upon the grand commercial empire built by the legendary group of merchants, we'll find that the footprints of these merchants are deeply imprinted on the road of humanity's new explorations in commercial civilization.

It stands as a commercial marvel born from the piling up of small increments, a treasured national legacy of being pragmatic and down-to-earth, a tangible embodiment of the wisdom of sizing up the situation and making the right decision.

Across centuries, they experienced both thriving and setbacks. They left deep traces in history, but they've never been away. The memories and traces left behind by them can still be found in all aspects of our life.

第三章　以义制利的独家秘诀

The Secret of Making an Ethical Profit

Part 3

中华文化强调"言必信，行必果"。讲诚信是中华民族的传统美德，也是晋商的鲜明标签。"言而有信、行为有诚、心中有敬"，最终成就了晋商商行天下的繁荣，尤其是晋商票号的兴起，创造性地建立了一套完善的信用制度体系。

Chinese culture emphasizes that "words must be believed, deeds must be fruitful". Honesty is the traditional virtue of the Chinese nation, and it is also the distinctive label of Jin merchants. "Words and letters, deeds are sincere, and there is respect in the heart", and finally achieved the prosperity of the Jin merchant firm in the world, especially the establishment of the Jin merchant ticket number, and creatively evolved a complete set of credit system.

手持魔杖、脚蹬一双长着翅膀的靴子。他，健步如飞、能言善辩、机敏过人。

他叫赫尔墨斯，爱马仕拿他的名字命名，国际花联用他的形象做标识，许多银行、船舶、航空公司围绕他设计品牌。他是古希腊神话中的"商业之神"，是西方人眼里妥妥的"男神"。

在古老的东方，华人世界，也有自己的"男神"，他就是与中国圣贤先师孔子齐名的武圣人关公。他是武功赫赫的"战神"，却被经商之人奉为"财神"，因为他是忠、义、仁、勇的化身，是信义与诚信的代表。

"信"，在东方价值体系中占据重要地位，"人无信不立"是中国人长期恪守的理念，也是中国商人历来秉持的核心价值。明清时期崛起的晋商，把同是山西人的关公奉为行业之神和精神领袖。关公崇拜也随着晋商不断扩大的商业版图走向世界，名重天下。关公"诚信仁义"的美德，被发扬成为诚实守信、以义制利的中国式商业文明。20 世纪初，一位英国汇丰银行的经理在离开上海回国前曾这样感慨："25 年来，与山西商人做了几亿两的巨额交易，没有遇到一个骗子。"

Holding a wand and wearing winged boots, he is fleet of foot, eloquent, as well as quick-witted.

West, Hermes. Hermes is named after him. Interflora uses his image as its logo. Many banks, shipbuilding companies, and airlines have designed brands inspired by him. He is the god of commerce in ancient Greek mythology and a true deity in the West.

In the East, Chinese people also have their own deity, Guan Yu, the martial god who is as highly esteemed as the paragon of Chinese sages, Confucius. He was the god of war with a great battle record, but businessmen always worship him as the god of wealth because he is the People praise him with the words of embodiment of righteousness and integrity.

Integrity occupies an important position in China's value system. Chinese people have long adhered to the philosophy that one cannot gain a foothold without integrity, which is also the core value that Chinese businessmen have always upheld. The Shanxi merchants who rose in the Ming and Qing dynasties worshipped Guan Yu, who was also from Shanxi, as the god of commerce and their spiritual leader. As Shanxi merchants continued to expand their business territory, the worship of Guan Yu was also spread all over the world. His virtue of integrity, benevolence, and righteousness was carried forward and then formed the Chinese business culture of emphasizing integrity and making only ethical profit. At the beginning of the 20th century, a manager of HSBC UK sighed before leaving Shanghai for home, "Over the past 25 years, I have conducted huge transactions worth hundreds of millions of taels of silver with Shanxi merchants, and I have not encountered a single scammer."

壹

"人在做，天在看。"这是中国人经常挂在嘴边的一句话。他们相信，善恶真假都逃不过抬头三尺神明的眼睛。早在 2700 多年前的春秋时期，当楚国人范蠡发明标准度量衡器杆秤时，就特意用天上的北斗七星和南斗六星作为计量符号。

一颗星为一两，每一两用一个黄色小点标记，代表秤星❶，意味着诚信。目的就是提醒经商之人，时时刻刻都要公平诚信地做买卖。秤在手中，义在心中。诚信经营，成为晋商行南走北的底气。

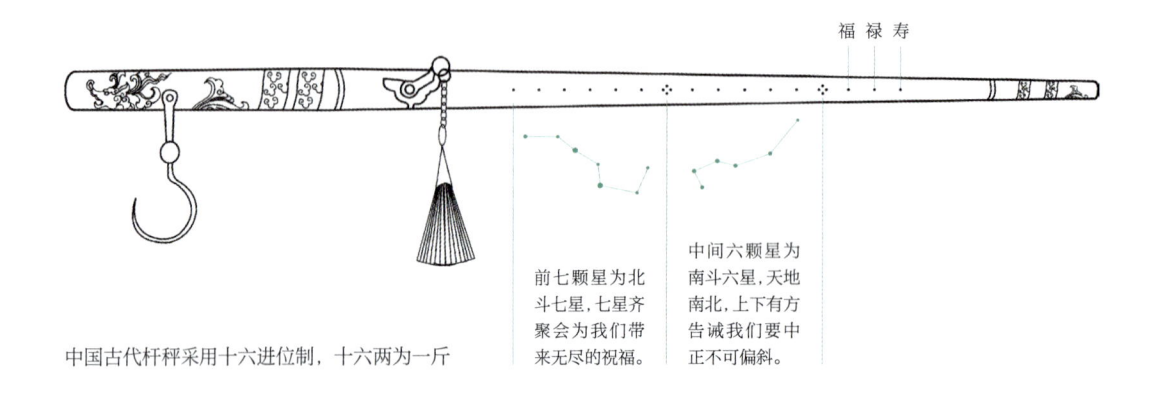

福 禄 寿

中国古代杆秤采用十六进位制，十六两为一斤

前七颗星为北斗七星，七星齐聚会为我们带来无尽的祝福。

中间六颗星为南斗六星，天地南北，上下有方告诫我们要中正不可偏斜。

秤星：秤杆上的刻度叫秤星，用在称量商品重量时作为标准。在民俗传说中，秤星被赋予了丰富的伦理内涵。古人将南斗六星，北斗七星，外加福禄寿三星共十六星，作为交易中的标准，即一斤，而每一颗星就是一两，所以一斤等于十六两。倘若短斤少两，少一两叫"损福"，少二两叫"伤禄"，少三两叫"折寿"。杆秤上的秤星必须是白色或黄色，不能用黑色，比喻做生意要公平、正直，不能黑心。

寻踪
晋商

乔家金街
Qiao Jia King Street

包头是内蒙古第二大城市，这座移民城市，到处彰显着山西气质。曾经，晋中乔家在包头开办了遍布全城的十几家"复"字商号，民间因此有了"先有复盛公，后有包头城"的传说。

清朝末年，包头城的乔家"复盛公"商号贴出了一张轰动全城的致歉信。事情的起因是分号的一家油坊把前一年剩下的棉籽油悄悄掺在了胡麻油中出售。

山西省晋商文化研究会会长　二级教授　刘建生

这件事被发现以后，乔财东采取了几个措施：第一处理涉事员工；第二现存的胡麻油全部销毁；第三已经售出的胡麻油予以赔偿。从此以后一传十、十传百，"复盛公"的名声大震，人们相信乔家

"复"字号，纷纷到"复"字号里买胡麻油，这显现了诚信的功能、作用和辐射力。

有德则有财。乔家的举动，虽损失了不少银钱，但却赢得了守信的美名。商人们因此更愿意与"复"字商号做买卖，"复"字商号的生意也越做越大。

山西财经大学晋商研究院院长　王书华

在商业的世界里，不能输的是信誉。以财富为研究对象的经济学家亚当·斯密，既写了一本《国富论》，又写了一本《道德情操论》，在后一本书里面他说道：不能把"富"与"道德"对立起来。可以说，信誉是商业之魂。

数百年前的一个个瞬间，被凝固在"走西口"的晋商群像中，雕刻着历史的表情。一座展陈晋商发展史的城市公园，被命名为"诚信主题公园"，也许在包头人看来，"诚信"二字，就是这些远道而来的山西商人最鲜明的标签。

清华大学中国经济史研究中心主任
中国商业史学会副会长　龙登高

中华商道在晋商地域商人群体当中表现得非常突出，也最为典型，

包头市诚信主题公园晋商雕像
Baotou city integrity theme park Jin Shang statue

甚至可以说发育程度是最高的。中华商道的核心是诚信与信用，突出地体现在契约精神，通过签订契约来达成交易，如果你不守信用，就会受到惩罚，如果你守信用，就会得到激励，所以契约精神也是晋商500年可持续发展的基础和支撑。

厦门大学历史与文化遗产学院教授
厦门大学历史研究所所长　林枫

商业文化里讲的诚信其实源于中华文化，中华文化最突出的表现就是儒家思想，儒家思想把诚信表达为"人而无信，不知其可"。诚信不是晋商独有的，但是晋商把诚信做到了极致。数百年来，晋商秉承"诚信"这个金字招牌，为自己带来了滚滚的财源。

1 /

A saying goes like this in China, "Gods are watching everything you do." They believe that gods can see everything happening in the world, good or evil, true or false. As early as 2,700 years ago during the Spring and Autumn Period, when Fan Li, a native of the State of Chu, invented the standard weighing instrument steelyard, he purposely used the 13 stars of the Big Dipper and Sagittarius as the symbol.

One star means one tael. One yellow point means one tael and it symbolizes integrity, serving to remind every merchant to conduct business fairly and honestly.

The steelyard is in the hand, while righteousness is in the heart. The insistence on fair and honest trading gave Shanxi merchants the confidence to expand their business throughout the country.

Baotou is the second largest city in Inner Mongolia. As a city of migrants, it's full of traces of Shanxi. The Qiao family from Jinzhong once had a dozen stores under the trade name Fu across Baotou, so a local saying goes that first came Fushenggong, then the city of Baotou.

In the late Qing Dynasty, the Qiao family's Fushenggong firm in Baotou posted an apology letter, which caused a sensation in the city. The cause of the matter was that an oil store of theirs mixed the cottonseed oil left over from the previous year into linseed oil to sell.

WANG SHUHUA, PRESIDENT
INSTITUTE OF SHANXI MERCHANT STUDIES,
SHANXI UNIVERSITY OF FINANCE AND
ECONOMICS
In the business world, one thing that is not to be lost is credibility.

寻踪
晋商

Adam Smith, an economist who studied wealth, wrote both The Wealth of Nations and The Theory of Moral Sentiments, in which he wrote that wealth and morality are not against each other, and credibility is actually the soul of commerce.

The moments from centuries ago are frozen in the portraits of the Shanxi merchants. This city park displaying the history of Shanxi merchants is named Integrity Theme Park. Perhaps for the people in Baotou, integrity is the most distinctive label of the Shanxi merchants who came from afar.

LONG DENGGAO
DIRECTOR OF CENTER FOR CHINESE ECONOMIC HISTORY, TSINGHUA UNIVERSITY
VICE PRESIDENT OF SOCIETY OF CHINESE COMMERCE HISTORY

It can be said that the Chinese business Tao is very prominent and the most typical among the merchant groups in the Jin Shang region, and it can even be said that the degree of development is the highest. Its core is integrity and credit, which is prominently reflected in the spirit of the contract, he is to conclude the transaction by signing the contract, if you do not keep your promises, you will be punished, if you keep your promises, you will be incentivized, so the spirit of the contract is also a foundation for the sustainable development of Jinshang for 500 years, a support.

LIN FENG
PROFESSOR AT SCHOOL OF HISTORY AND CULTURAL HERITAGE, XIAMEN UNIVERSITY
DIRECTOR OF INSTITUTE OF HISTORY, XIAMEN UNIVERSITY

Integrity in business culture originated from the Chinese culture, mainly Confucianism, which interprets integrity as one cannot achieve anything without it. Shanxi merchants were not the only group that emphasized integrity, but they pushed it to its extreme. Over centuries, they held high the philosophy of integrity and developed very successful businesses.

贰

现在我们赚了钱可以存银行,可是古代没有银行,手里的真金白银既占地方又抢眼,怎么办?其实,古代也有一个可以存钱的地方,就是票号,只不过与银行把钱放在保险柜里不同的是,很多票号会在地下挖个大金库,存放体积庞大的金银。

在平遥城一处地下有一座金库,近300平方米的空间里,10间窑洞排列两侧。这么一座大金库出现在一个小县城里,真是低调的奢华!有人测算过,如果把这里所能容储的黄金白银换算成人民币,相当于300亿元。可问题是,当时个人征信与社会信用

协同庆钱庄地下金库
Cooperate to celebrate the bank underground vault

制度都极不完善，那些财富的所有者们，凭什么就敢把大笔大笔的血汗钱交给别人来经营保管呢？如果经营不善，赔了算谁的？

> **山西省晋商文化研究会常务理事　张宪平**
> 为什么人们敢把钱存到票号呢？有这么几个原因：第一，票号成立的时候，它就有同业的信誉担保；第二，从经营管理上来讲，它是有无限责任承诺的，如果经营不好赔了钱，不怕还不了钱。就是说父亲经营不好儿子还，儿子还不完孙子还。总之一定会保护储户的利益。

> **美国籍媒体评论员　托马斯·鲍肯二世**
> 商业诚信是所有商业活动的关键，因此在山西，随着汇票的发展，晋商担保会妥善储存人们账户里的钱财。这些钱财不仅能在山西省内取用，而且还能从他们的分号行支取，不仅是中国其他地区的分号，甚至包括日本、新加坡、俄罗斯的分号，这种类型的担保是我们今天看到的真正的银行系统的关键所在。晋商是构筑当今银行体系的重要先驱之一。

这种无限责任，成就了晋商经营史上至今可圈可点的"东掌互信"●制度。晋商票号采取所有权与经营权分离的"东伙合作"模式，也称"东掌制度"。东家虽然是出资人，但却把经营权全部交给非亲非故的大掌柜。一

东掌制度
East control system

❶ 东掌制度：山西商人的一种经营管理制度。财东凭信义出资聘请掌柜来主责经营。所聘掌柜在号内拥有决策、设置分号、录用职工、调配人员等权力。财东也受号规约束，如财东平时不得在号内住宿、借钱、指挥号内人为其办事等，只享有年底结账时对掌柜的任免权。这样，掌柜可以最大限度地调动人、财、物等，达到最高经营水平。

切用人作业，全体伙计听命于掌柜，东家从不过问。可一旦营业失败，经济损失却全由财东负担。东家凭信义出资聘请掌柜主责经营，掌柜以诚信和业绩回报财东，东家和掌柜用彼此信任签订了相互合作的牢固契约。

山西省晋商文化研究会常务理事　张宪平

"东掌制度"实际上是一种信托制度，用我们现在的话讲，就是所有权和经营权相分离，这也是晋商商业智慧的体现。它的基础是出资者和经营者之间必须肝胆相照、双向信任，这也是晋商诚实守信精神的一种体现。

"信"是信仰、信念，是一种精神力量。山西商人把这种精神力量转化成支撑经营的商业价值，从诚信理念中，创造性地建立了一套完善的信用制度体系，让精神世界的信仰，穿透商界的欺诈错讹，成为一种可以操作的有效规则。

在民间，曾流传着晋商巨富曹家与掌柜之间用人不疑的故事。当年，曹家在沈阳开设富森峻商号时，掌柜领取了7万两白银作本金，谁知出师不利，赔得一干二净。掌柜向东家报告亏赔的经过，东家认为他讲得非常有道理，不仅没有责怪，反而问他是否还敢干。掌柜说只要东家信任，当然敢干，于是掌柜领到第二笔资本再赴沈阳。不料几年之后，又赔光了，东家又付给他第三笔资本。深受知遇之恩的掌柜感激万分，三闯关东，这一次，他不仅赢回了前几次的亏赔，而且以盈余在沈阳又开设了4个分号。从此曹家资本大为扩张，利润大为增长。

曹家金火车头钟
Cao Jiajin locomotive bell

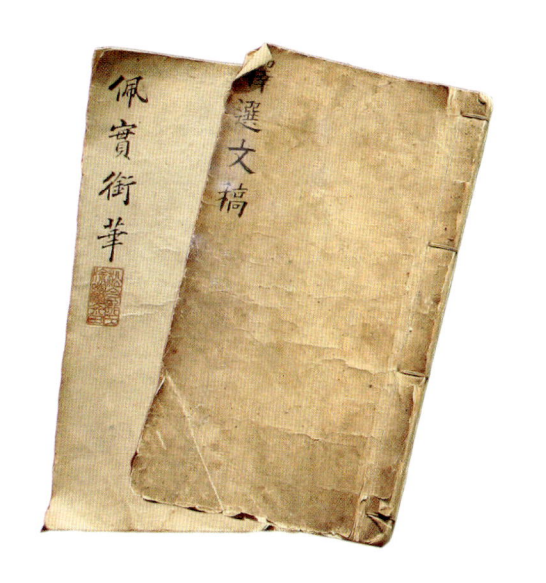

《劝号谱》清代时期晋商抄写的做合格商人和经商应注意的事项抄写本
Advice No Qing Dynasty Jin businessmen copied to do qualified businessmen and business should pay attention to the matters copied

在中国商业史上，山西商人是所有权和经营权分离的最早实践者。直到100多年后的公元1932年，西方经济学者才提出"两权分离"的概念。

厦门大学历史与文化遗产学院教授

厦门大学历史研究所所长　林枫

晋商在职业经理人这一点上，也就是现代公司制度方面，走在了时代的最前沿，东家当时只有两个权力，出钱的权力和选掌柜的权力。东家掏钱选掌柜，选了掌柜之后其它事情一概交给掌柜，东家甚至连推荐学徒的权力都没有。所有的用人用钱，都是由掌柜来负责。

蔚盛長號規

票號分號人員，無論出門路途之遠近，統以三年為一班期，除遇父母喪葬大事外，不得輕易告假，每月準寄平安家信，但不得私寄銀錢及物品，一切舉動辦事，悉承總號命令。

尚有特別禁條：

第一、不准接眷出外。
第二、不准在外娶妻納妾。
第三、不准宿娼賭博。
第四、不准在外開設商店。
第五、不准捐納實職官銜。
第六、不准攜帶親故在外謀事。

大盛魁號規

號內人員一律不准攜帶家眷。
號內人員不得長髮短鬚。
號內財物不得挪用。
號享單干不合作。
號內人員不得兼營其它業得。
禁止賭錢吸食鴉片。
號內人員不得與外人銀錢來往。
不得請個人親戚朋友，不得利用東和掌櫃家具闖官司。
號內人員非因號事不得會朋，由字號內統一慶賀禮儀，贈員不得飛觴飲席，不相送禮。
號內人員不得私自囤積貨物，相互走親。
號內人員亦不得互拉拢揽，以相謀生。
不得在外兼差，不兼官職。
號內人員以上下清況之一，立即開除出號，行業門規，絲毫學和，不絕提握揮揖勒舍。

大德通票號號規

各碼頭地方，難免有賭錢之風，壞品失節，鋪累籍外，老少人等，一概不准，犯者初出，劃不容緩，難免敗光，嚴之禁之。

各號頭凡諸號錢盤，買空賣空諸事，大許號禁，倘有犯者，立刻出號，人力效用，一度至六度，四年清結，七度至一度（十度），六年清結，若約頂身股，未縱睽期而放者，勿論多少，三年清結，若功績異常，或臨放有效之事，宜加宜誠，京東另議。

蔚字五聯號庚子后條規

一、近年以來商務盛行，未閱之利人尚遺之若，蒙若莉息也有私和寡欺者，請位號友能毋努力。
一、各莘利息也有私和寡欺者，我伙息頭知恩之。
一、各緊倒賬除實高利借貸，倘因不自投該，重則出號，輕則罰俸，不俗外原情。
一、各莊宴會叫戲，各老板皆此就挑回銀錢，混費多多，此後不遇藉以消遣，號中懸然聚賭，查即禁止。
一、號伙衣服已屬華豪，而又窮奢極欲，更求精潔，此殖風欲不唯自己折福，凡聽聞者，莫不痛恨，且易為外人所忌，除實系本高帶病，資格深大者不准，如有外嫖欺女人者，定行嚴究。

晋商号规
Shanxi merchants number regulations

万金账：完整的万金账通常包括《合约》、《号规》和《股权收益》三个部分。《合约》是由合伙各财东与掌柜签订的协议文书，是股权合作关系正规化、制度化、契约化的表现，使拥有财股或身股各方的利益得到制度认可和保证。《合约》规定了出资人与经营层各自的权利和义务，是代理委托关系的基石。《号规》类似于《公司章程》，既使掌柜的经营管理纳入正规化、制度化的轨道，同时也使一般员工的权益得到了制度上的保障。《股权收益》记录了财股和身股的股份和每个账期分红等财务信息，反映了票号的股份构成以及各个股东在财务上的权益。万金账的建立标志着山西商人治理结构制度体系的形成，它在山西商人发展史上和中国金融发展史上，都占有极其重要的地位。

信任，是企业的重要资本。现代企业制度讲究充分授权、信任管理，而早在300多年前的山西商人，就已经在多年打拼的经验和教训中深刻领悟了这个道理，并将其具化成一套行之有效的经营管理制度。他们用严格的员工选拔和培养机制，把诚信这一经商法宝，从入职之初就牢牢扎根在每一个票号人心中，内化为日常的行为准则。

19世纪末的一个寻常日子，一名小伙计刚进票号第一天，就无意间从墙角扫到一些细碎银钱。想来应该是柜上不慎掉落的，他便马上交到了柜上。可第二天扫地时，他竟再次捡到了银钱，照样如数交还了。接下来的一段时间，小学徒总能隔三差五扫到一些细碎银钱。尽管偶尔也会有私藏起来的念头，但每一次都只是一闪而过，最后还是如数交还了。多年后，这个细致勤快、诚实纯良的小伙计已升任票号三掌柜。其实，当年那些碎银两，正是对他人品的考量。如果当时他把这些碎银据为己有，换来的将会是一个言辞婉转的辞退令。可这位小伙计，干活儿仔细又拾金不昧，所以成功拿到了品优心正的考核评价。

这样的场景，在各家票号和商行里经过不同版本的演绎，成为晋商选人用人的第一道门槛。然而无论是哪种方式的考验，答案都只有一个，那就是：想要在山西商号当伙计，首先得是一个诚实的人。

山西财经大学晋商研究院院长　王书华

中国人历来秉承一个理念：商道即人道。做事先做人，清白守信是商号对伙计的基本要求。晋商在长期的经营实践中，逐渐形成了一套以"诚信"为核心的严谨规范的员工选聘机制。掌柜对应聘者祖上三代的职业、德性要进行严格考察；招聘员工要实行举荐制和担保制，一旦违反号规，担保人要负责任；伙计一旦犯了错误被开除后，其他分号也不会录用。

"寒窗十年考状元，学商十年倍加难"，为了使员工具备无可挑剔的职业操守和专业能力，商号要对他们进行严格的培训和长时间的考核磨练。"重信用、除虚伪、敦品行、贵忠诚、鄙利己、奉博爱"的商业道德和做人准则，更是作为一项终身教育，渗透在员工们日复一日的工作生活中。

伙计诚信与"东掌互信"，共同夯实了晋商信用体系的制度基石。因此，损害票号的谋私行为极少发生，甚至"舞弊情事，百年不遇"。而这套科学严谨的信用体系，又如同一个用制度织就的细密筛子，把全社会最有奋斗热情、最具职业精神、最富诚信品格的出色人才筛选了出来。从晋商商号走出去的，是一个个神采奕奕、承载着中华商业精神的优秀职业经理人。他们用诚实守信这张汇通天下的"汇票"，书写了一段又一段商业传奇。

平遥古城街景
Pingyao ancient city street view

2

Nowadays, we can bank the money we earn, but there weren't banks in ancient times. Then how to deal with the space-consuming and eye-catching gold and silver? In fact, in ancient times, there was also a place where you could store money, which is Piaohao, or private banks. The difference is that banks put the money in safes, but many Piaohao would dig a large underground vault to store the space-consuming gold and silver.

This is the former site of an underground vault in Pingyao. In this space of nearly 300 square meters, ten caves are lined up on both sides. Such a large vault in a small county town can only be described as low-key luxury. Some have calculated that if the gold and silver stored here are converted into renminbi, it is equivalent to 30 billion yuan.

But the question is, at that time, the personal and social credit systems were extremely imperfect, so why would people dare to give their hard-earned money to others for management and safekeeping? Who would be responsible for any losses incurred in the event of mismanagement?

There were several reasons why people dared to deposit their money in these private banks. First, when a private bank was established, peers would vouch for it with their credibility. Second, from the perspective of operation and management, private banks had unlimited liability. In other words, even if a private bank lost money due to poor management, it would still return the depositors' money in full with interest. The son would pay the father's debt, and if the son couldn't get it done, the grandson would continue to do so. They would do whatever it takes to protect the interests of depositors.

There is no doubt that business integrity is the key to all business activities, so in Shanxi, with the development of bills of exchange, Jin Shang guarantees will properly store the money in people's accounts, which can not only be used in Shanxi Province, but also from their branches, not only in other parts of China, but even in Japan, Singapore, Russia, this type of guarantee is the key to the real banking system that we see today. I will find that Jinshang is one of the important pioneers in building today's banking system.

This kind of unlimited liability also accomplished the Owner and Manager system, which is still remarkable in the business history of Shanxi merchants.

Shanxi private banks were mainly operated in the Owner and Manager model, in which ownership and management rights were separated. The owner was the funder, but management rights belonged to the manager. The manager had full authority over the store, and the owner wouldn't interfere. If the business was not well run, the financial loss would be borne by the owner. Out of trust, the owner hired the manager to run the business, and in return, the manager would run the business with integrity and make it grow. Mutual trust allowed the owner and the manager to build a strong partnership.

ZHANG XIANPING, MANAGING DIRECTOR
SHANXI MERCHANTS CULTURE RESEARCH
ASSOCIATION OF SHANXI PROVINCE

The Owner and Manager system was actually a trust system, which is called today the separation of ownership and management rights. It was also a reflection of the business wisdom of Shanxi merchants. So, what was the basis of it? It was the mutual trust between the owner and the manager, which was also an embodiment of Shanxi merchants' adherence to honesty and integrity.

Integrity was faith, belief, and a kind of spiritual power. Shanxi merchants turned this spiritual power into a commercial value to support the business. Through the philosophy of integrity, they creatively developed a mature credit system, allowing spiritual faith and belief to curb fraudulent actions in the business world and become effective and practical rules.

There was once a story about the Cao family, a very wealthy merchant family in Shanxi, who gave the manager their complete trust.

Back then, when the Cao family opened a private bank named Fusenjun in Shenyang, the manager received 70,000 taels of silver as start-up capital. But it didn't work well and all the money went down in drain. The manager reported the process to the owner, and the owner thought that everything he said made sense. Instead of blaming the manager, the owner asked him whether he dared to try again. The manager said of course as long as the owner could still trust him. Then he went to Shenyang with start-up capital again. However, it was all lost again after a few years, and the owner gave him a third chance. Deeply grateful for the kindness of the owner, the manager made his third trip to Shenyang. This time, he not only earned back the previous losses, but also used the profit to open four branches in Shenyang. From then on, the Cao family's business started to grow greatly, and so did the profit.

In China's business history, Shanxi merchants were the first practitioners of the separation of ownership and management rights. It was not until 1932, more than 100 years later, that the concept of the separation of ownership and management rights was first introduced in Western economics.

> **LIN FENG**
> **PROFESSOR AT SCHOOL OF HISTORY AND CULTURAL HERITAGE, XIAMEN UNIVERSITY**

DIRECTOR OF INSTITUTE OF HISTORY, XIAMEN UNIVERSITY

He was at the forefront of the times in terms of professional managers, in terms of the modern company system, and the owner only had two powers at that time, what power? The right to pay money, the right to choose the treasurer. You pay for the shopkeeper, and after you choose the shopkeeper, everything else will be handed over to the shopkeeper, and the owner doesn't even have the right to recommend apprentices. The complete employment of people and money is the responsibility of the shopkeeper.

Trust is an important asset of the enterprise. Modern enterprise system emphasizes full authorization and trust management, while as early as 300 years ago, Shanxi merchants already had a profound understanding of it from years of business experience and turned it into an effective business management system. In this system, the staff selection and training mechanism made integrity, the core value of business, firmly rooted in the heart of every employee from the very beginning of their employment, becoming their daily code of conduct.

One day in the late 19th century, a clerk, who just started his first day at the private bank, inadvertently noticed some scattered silver in the corner during cleaning. He thought it must have fallen off the counter, so he immediately handed it back. But on the next day, he found some silver on the ground again when sweeping the floor, and he returned it again. Over the next period of time, the young man could find some silver every now and then. Although occasionally he had passing thoughts of keeping it for himself, he always returned it in the end.

Years later, this meticulous, diligent, and honest clerk became the third-in-command of the private bank. In fact, those scattered silver was the test of his character. If he had kept the silver for himself, he would have gotten a polite letter of dismissal. But this clerk was careful in work and upright in conduct, so he was judged to be of good character.

All the private banks and stores had tests like this. The tests served as the first threshold when Shanxi merchants were about to appoint, select, and employ people. But no matter what the form of the tests was, the answer was the same. That is, you must be an honest person to work for Shanxi merchants.

> **WANG SHUHUA, PRESIDENT**
> **INSTITUTE OF SHANXI MERCHANT STUDIES, SHANXI**
> **UNIVERSITY OF FINANCE AND ECONOMICS**
> Chinese people have always believed that the key to business success lies in being a righteous person. Honesty and integrity were the basic requirements for employees. In their long-term business practices, Shanxi merchants gradually formed a rigorous and standardized system for staff selection and recruitment with integrity as the core. The owner would scrutinize the occupation and morality of the three generations of the applicant's family. The recruitment of staff was based on a recommendation policy and a surety system. In the event that an employee violated the rules, the surety would take full responsibility. Once an employee made mistakes and got fired, he wouldn't be hired by any branch.

"One needs to study hard for ten years to do well in the imperial examination, and learning to do business is even much harder. "In order to ensure that employees had impeccable ethics and professionalism, firms would train them rigorously and hone their skills over a long period of time. The business ethics and code of conduct of emphasizing integrity, eliminating hypocrisy, upholding morality, valuing loyalty, despising self-interest, and practicing benevolence were permeated in the daily work and life of employees as a lifelong education.

Honest employees and the mutual trust between the owner and the manager together solidified the foundation of Shanxi merchants' credit system. Therefore, very few people took advantage of their positions to seek personal gains in the private banks. It's said that there wouldn't be more than one fraud in a century.

This scientific and rigorous credit system was like a fine sieve woven by the system, selecting the outstanding talents with passion, professionalism, and honesty from the whole society. Shanxi merchants cultivated numerous excellent professional managers, who were full of vigor and carried forward the Chinese business culture. With honesty and integrity, a money order that could be cashed all over the world, they wrote down their own legend of business.

叁

试想一下，当年客户把沉甸甸的银子抬进来，转身出门时却只带走这样一张薄薄的汇票。一纸信符，何以承载万两白银？其实除了"诚比金坚"的道德承诺，还有一项高科技的加持。

印钞防伪技术，一项被誉为"仅次于原子弹的机密"，在全

中国票号博物馆（日昇昌票号）馆藏汇票
China Ticket number Museum (Rishengchang ticket number) collection money order

球200多个国家中，只有34个国家能够掌握。作为全球最大印钞国，中国就曾为十几个国家代印钞票。而早在200多年前，山西商人就用他们的"土科技"，破解了汇票的防伪技术。

左图中这张汇票的尾端，有一串类似密语的文字——"章善看流通"，晦涩难懂。它们究竟暗藏着什么样的玄机呢？

日昇昌的墙上有这样一幅字："谨防假票冒取，勿忘细视书章"，这句话看似是在叮嘱伙计，其实另有玄机。这12个汉字代表了12个月份。这首六句五言诗——"到头必分明，善恶总有报。阴谋害他人，昧心图自利。天道最公平，堪笑世情薄。"正好30个字，代表每个月的1日到30日。"生客多察看，斟酌而后行"，这10个汉字正好代表了阿拉伯数字1到10。而"国宝流通"4个字，则对应万、千、百、两这4个位数。据说这样的密押有400多组，定期来回替换。所以这张汇票上的"章善看流通"，密码内容结合票面信息翻译过来就是：道光二十六年十二月二十一日汇入北京500两，取兑日期是第二年的正月二十一。

汇票密押
Secret deposit of bills of exchange

寻踪
晋商

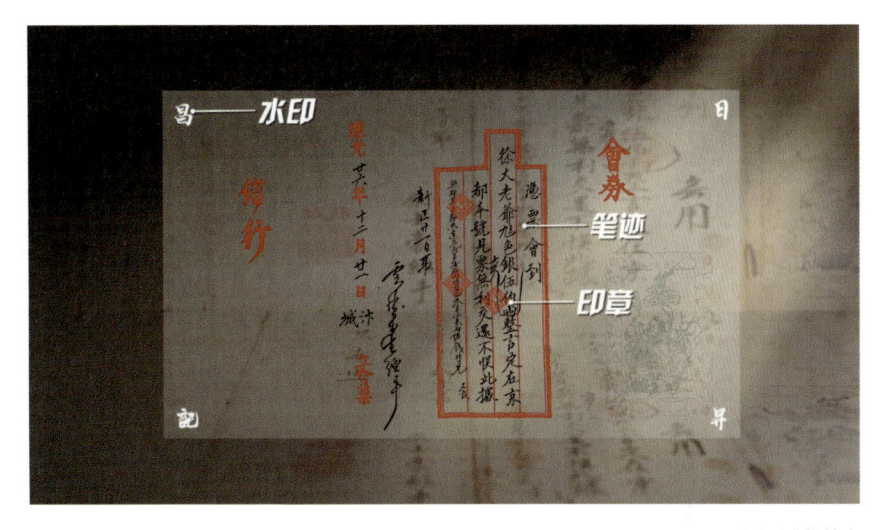

汇票防伪技术
Anti-counterfeiting technology of bills of exchange

密押防伪，只是汇票四重防伪技术之一。一张汇票，同时还要用笔迹、印章和水印来确保防伪。正是这套被称为"山西商人智慧4.0版"的防伪技术，让百年老号日昇昌没有发生过一起冒领错领事件。

> **北京大学经济学院经济史学系主任**
> **中国经济思想史学会副会长　周建波**
> 中国的文化为汇票的保密创造了条件，密码经常换，不然久了大家就会破译。中国的唐诗宋词很多，可以一个月，甚至半个月换一套密码，外人是很难去破解的。

如果说"东掌互信"和员工诚信是晋商诚信经营的体制性因素，那么

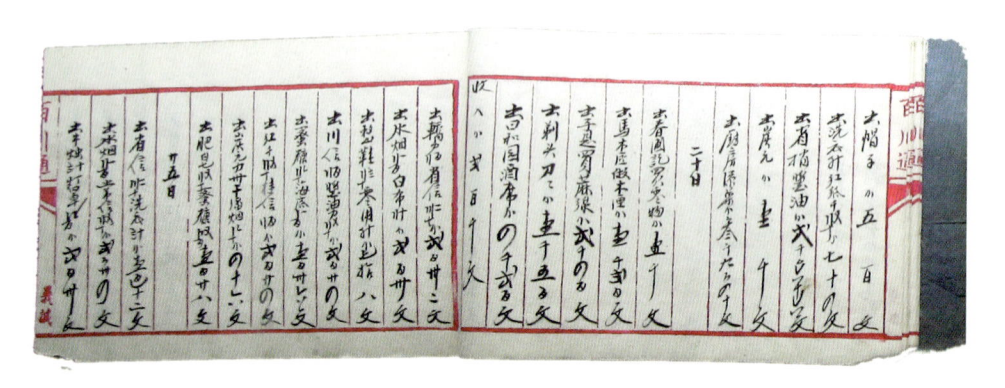

百川通票号核算清账账本（1880 年）
Baichuantong Bill Number Accounting and Settlement Account Book (1880)

汇票防伪技术，则为维护良好的商业信誉提供了机制性保障。

民国年间，著名经济学家马寅初曾对票号的历史贡献做出这样的评价："如是既无长途运现之烦，又无中途水火盗贼之险，而收解又可两清。商业之兴，国富以增，票庄历史上贡献不可谓不大。"而这样的巨大贡献，正是来自这些诚实与精明兼修双备的山西商人。他们身着长袍马褂，从历史的深处走来，带给我们智慧的启迪与精神的力量。

3

This is a money order collected in Rishengchang Museum. Just imagine that customers came here with a lot of silver and left only with a thin piece of paper. What made a piece of paper equivalent to thousands of taels of silver? In addition to the merchants' promise, a piece of high technology made it possible.

The anti-counterfeit technology used in banknote printing is described as "second only to the atomic bomb in terms of classification level", which is only mastered by 34 countries out of more than 200 countries and regions in the world. As the world's largest banknote printing country, China has printed banknotes for a dozen countries. But 200 years ago, Shanxi merchants already achieved the anti-counterfeiting of money orders with their technology.

At the end of this money order is a string of obscure characters that look like ciphers. What kind of secret does it conceal?

There is a line on the wall of Rishengchang, "Beware of counterfeit money orders and always examine the seal carefully. " It may look like just a reminder to the clerks, but it's much more than that. These Chinese characters stand for the 12 months. This five-character poem with six lines contains 30 characters, each of which symbolizes a day in a month. "Pay extra attention to unfamiliar customers, and think thoroughly before taking action. " This line represents numbers from 1 to 10, beside which is the alternative version. The four characters Guobaoliutong, meaning the circulation of national treasures, are for ten-thousands place, thousands place, hundreds place, and taels respectively. It's said that there were more than 400 sets of such test keys, which were regularly rotated. Now look at this money order in my hand. According to the test keys that we just saw, it means that 500 taels of silver was remitted to Beijing on the 21st day of the 12th lunar month in 1846, and that the withdrawal date was the 21st day of the first lunar month of the next year.

The test keys were just one of the four pieces of anti-counterfeiting technologies for money orders. The other three were handwriting verification, seals, and watermarks. It was this set of anti-counterfeiting technologies that prevented the century-old Rishengchang from having even a single false claim.

> ZHOU JIANBO
> DIRECTOR OF DEPARTMENT OF ECONOMIC HISTORY, SCHOOL OF ECONOMICS, PEKING UNIVERSITY
> VICE PRESIDENT OF CHINA SOCIETY FOR THE HISTORY OF ECONOMIC THOUGHTS
> Chinese culture made it possible to realize anti-counterfeiting this way because the test keys could be changed very often. There are so many poems that the merchants could change the test keys monthly or even semimonthly, which made it very difficult to crack the code.

If the mutual trust between owners and managers and the integrity of employees were the institutional factors that allowed Shanxi merchants to run business honestly, the anti-counterfeiting technologies of money orders provided technical support for maintaining a good business reputation.

Ma Yinchu, a famous economist in the period of the Republic of China, once said this about the historical contribution of Piaohao, or private banks, "Private banks saved people the trouble of transporting silver over long distances, eliminated risks such as water, fire, and theft, and made payment easy and clear. The growth of the country's wealth relies on the prosperity of commerce, so private banks' historical contribution is enormous. "And such a great contribution came from these honest and shrewd Shanxi merchants. Dressed in robes and mandarin jackets, they came from the depths of history, bringing us endless wisdom and spiritual power.

肆

在平遥有句俗语："填不满的平遥城，银子元宝绊倒人。"这些真金白银，大部分是在外经商的山西商人委托镖局运送回来的。

在晋商开辟的商业版图中，镖局，以始终不可或缺的保护作用，写下了一段段精彩的江湖传奇。

早期，从我国东南沿海到蒙古乃至欧洲的远途贩运商队，离不开镖师的万里护佑；后期，现银的地区调配、总分号之间的物资往来，离不开镖局的物流疏通。每商必镖，有晋商的地方就一定有山西镖局的足迹。史料记载，仅 1906 年到 1921 年间，北京的镖局就多达 20 余家。而商家与镖局之间，是财货相托，更是生死相依。

《又见平遥》情境剧就讲述了一个票号与镖局之间生死相托、血脉相融的故事。清朝末期，平遥古城票号分号王掌柜一家罹难沙俄，仅留下一子做人质，对方提出，用 30 万两白银才能赎回。为接回王家仅存血脉，票号东家赵易硕抵尽家产，雇佣 232 名镖师一同前往沙俄接人，一走就是整整 7 年。其间赵东家途中遇难，全体镖师也以性命为代价，信守了镖局对票号的承诺。王家之子终于回归故里，血脉存续。

山西财经大学晋商研究院院长　王书华

商家把镖交给镖局，就相当于把性命交给了镖局，这中间

《又见平遥》剧照
A still from Pingyao Again

靠的是"信","信"字体现出镖局具备了中国传统文化中的忠义品质。这种忠义品质有两种含义：一是"士为知己者死"；二是"其言必信，其行必果，已诺必诚"。

在平遥南大街的镖局博物馆里，几乎每一个匾额上都少不了"义"字。当商家把自己的身家性命交给镖局的那一刻起，镖师也把比自己生命还要重的名誉交给了商家。命可以丢，但押镖的货物不能丢，信义不能丢。否则一次失手，就能让镖局身败名裂，永远无法立足于江湖之上。

"忠义勇"匾额
"Loyalty and courage" plaque

镖师
Armed escort

寻踪
晋商

千里行镖，天下晋商。从某种意义上讲，晋商的信誉，是勇武忠义的镖师们用生命在维系。因此，当清朝末年晋商票号在风雨飘摇中黯然落幕时，镖行江湖的传奇也逐渐在历史舞台上消失了。

19世纪末20世纪初，外国银行纷纷登陆中国，清朝政府也萌生了组建国有银行的想法。公元1905年清政府组建大清户部银行，公元1908年户部银行改组为大清银行。其间两次邀请山西票号入股经营，但都被拒绝了。

山西大学经济与管理学院教授　博士生导师　石涛

1895年签订《马关条约》之后，中国的民族资产阶级开始崛起，他们开始大量地投资近代企业。近代企业的成长需要一个新的金融机构来完成对它们的投资，但票号是不具备这种功能的，因为它服务的对象是传统的商业。从某种意义上讲，它的放款功能是非常微弱的，已经不适应整个社会的发展了。

就这样，穿马褂的票号掌柜，被着西装的银行经理不断挤压着生存空间，就连"天下第一号"的日昇昌也日渐衰微。公元1914年10月，"天下票号之首"的日昇昌宣布破产的大新闻轰动中国商界，"彼巍巍灿烂之华屋，无不铁扉双锁，黯淡无色……"。

寻踪
晋商

中国镖局博物馆
China Biaoju Museum

山西省晋商文化研究会常务理事　张宪平

日昇昌倒闭的直接导火索，是它的北京分号为欠下巨额债务的祁县合盛元作担保而受到牵连。当时日昇昌北京分号的资产被查封了，平遥总号的资产也被清查了，甚至东家都被扣押了。

危急时刻，早已辞职归乡的日昇昌总号前任二掌柜梁怀文重新出山，自告奋勇，赴京解救票号危急。他一面竭尽全力用自己在业内的声望和信誉，说服在京的72家债权人联名公禀，请司法部暂停破产执行；一面派人到各地清理账务。经过长达8年的清理整顿，公元1922年，日昇昌票号复业了，但却再也没有恢复其往日的辉煌，勉强维持了10年后，最终停止了百余年的票号事业。

正是这位本来可以置身事外的梁怀文，靠着救人于危难的侠义，为日昇昌票号挽回了最后一口元气。用他入职票号时掌柜对东家的承诺，守住了日昇昌票号"言而有信"的荣誉。

北京大学经济学院经济史学系主任
中国经济思想史学会副会长　周建波

票号是无限责任公司，银行是有限责任公司。日昇昌票号，包括以日昇昌为代表的晋商，一个票号垮了，会把它所有产业都带垮。所以不同的业态，在面对战争、动乱、危机时，优劣势就显示出来了。

20世纪初,军阀混战、局势动荡,中华大地生灵涂炭、民不聊生,山西票号的经营也受到了影响。辛亥革命后,原先分布在全国城镇的500多座票号,到公元1917年已减少到不足40座。这时,如果晋商放弃以义制利的原则,唯利是图,完全可以趁乱大发横财,扭转败局。然而,在生死存亡之际,山西商人几乎是集体选择了舍生取义。

20世纪30年代,因中原大战失利,由山西省银行印发的晋钞大幅贬值。为扭转金融混乱的局面,改组后的山西省银行发行了兑换券,也就是新币,以1∶25的比例回收市面上的晋钞。当时,许多票号都经营着晋钞

山西银行旧址
Former site of Shanxi Bank

的存放款业务，如果对存款户以晋钞支付，储户的存款就贬值了，而票号却可以发一笔横财。但他们却没有选择这种损人利己的不义之法，而是反其道而行之，对晋钞存款户以新币付出。这样，储户的存款保值了，而票号却赔钱了。

"宁叫赔折腰，不让客吃亏。"为了维护商誉，大多数山西票号都选择了自己咽下晋钞贬值的苦，以至于亏空越来越大，再也无力回天。日薄西山，铁扉锁住了"汇通天下"的票号辉煌。但一代代晋商"忠义为魂、诚信为本"的精神之光，却穿透紧闭的门扉，熠熠闪亮。

4

A saying went like this in Pingyao, "Pingyao can never be filled, and people might trip over the silver all around the city." Most of the silver was brought back by escort agencies commissioned by Shanxi merchants doing business away from home.

In the commercial territory opened up by Shanxi merchants, the escort agencies have written their wonderful legends with their indispensable roles as escorts.

In the early days, the caravans traveling long distances from the southeastern coast to Mongolia and Europe needed the service of escort agencies along the way. In the later period, the regional deployment of silver and the exchange of materials between the branches couldn't be done without escort agencies. Every business trip needed to be escorted, so where there were Shanxi merchants, there were Shanxi escort agencies.

According to historical records, there were more than 20 escort agencies in Beijing between 1906 and 1921. The escort agencies were responsible for the safety of the merchants and their properties, and they would fulfill their duties no matter the cost. The immersive play Pingyao Once More tells a story between a private bank and an escort agency.

In the late Qing Dynasty, Manager Wang of a private bank in Pingyao was killed in Russia together with his family, and only one of his sons was kept alive and held as a hostage. The kidnappers demanded a ransom of 300,000 taels of silver. To keep the last descendant of the Wang family alive, Zhao Yishuo, the owner of the private bank, spent every penny he had and hired 232 escorts to bring him back from Russia, which took seven whole years. At last, at the cost of all the escorts' lives, the escort agency fulfilled its commitment to the private bank. Zhao Yishuo also sacrificed his own life to keep the son of Manager Wang alive.

WANG SHUHUA, PRESIDENT
INSTITUTE OF SHANXI MERCHANTS STUDIES, SHANXI
UNIVERSITY OF FINANCE AND ECONOMICS
So when the merchants had the escort agency deliver silver, it was equivalent to trusting their lives to the agency, and they would do it because of trust and integrity. This shows that escort agencies had two qualities highlighted in traditional Chinese culture, loyalty and integrity. They would die for those who trusted and appreciated them, and they would keep their promises regardless of the cost.

In the Escort Agency Museum on the Nandajie Street in Pingyao, the word righteousness is on almost every plaque. When the merchants trusted their lives to the escort agency, the escorts would stake their reputation, which was even more valuable than their lives, to get the job done. Lives can be lost, but not the goods escorted. Otherwise, a single failure would ruin the escort agency's reputation and make it never able to rise again.

The escort agencies were always with Shanxi merchants. In a sense, the credibility of Shanxi merchants was maintained by the brave and loyal escorts with their lives. Therefore, when private banks of Shanxi met their gloomy end in the late Qing Dynasty, the legend of the escort agencies also faded away in history.

Since the mid-19th century, foreign banks landed in China one after another, and the Qing government also developed the idea of establishing a state-owned bank. In 1905, the Qing government founded the Great Qing Bank of the Ministry of Revenue. In 1908, it was reorganized into the Great Qing Government Bank. During that period, Shanxi merchants rejected the proposal to join hands twice.

寻踪
晋商

PROF. SHI TAO, DOCTORAL SUPERVISOR
SCHOOL OF ECONOMICS AND MANAGEMENT, SHANXI UNIVERSITY

After the signing of the Treaty of Shimonoseki in 1895, China's national bourgeoisie began to rise, or awaken, and began to invest heavily in modern enterprises. The growth of modern enterprises requires a new financial institution to complete the investment in modern enterprises. Under such a premise, the ticket number does not have such a function, because the object of its service is the traditional enterprise, the traditional business, in a sense, its lending function is very weak, that is, the loan function is very weak, under such a premise, the ticket number has not adapted to the development of the whole society.

The living space of the Piaohao managers in mandarine jackets was constantly squeezed by the bank managers in suits, and even Rishengchang, known as the World's No. 1 Piaohao, was declining. In October 1914, the news of Rishengchang declaring bankruptcy caused a sensation throughout China's business community. "All those magnificent and splendid houses are now locked up. All their charm and colors are gone."

ZHANG XIANPING, MANAGING DIRECTOR
SHANXI MERCHANTS CULTURE RESEARCH ASSOCIATION OF SHANXI PROVINCE

The immediate trigger for the closure of Rishengchang was that its Beijing branch was involved as a guarantor for Heshengyuan in Qixian County, which owed huge debts. At that time, the assets of Rishengchang's Beijing branch were seized, and so were its assets in the headquarters in Pingyao. Even its owner was in custody.

At this critical moment, Liang Huaiwen, the long-retired former second-in-command of the headquarters of Rishengchang, volunteered to go to Beijing to save the firm in crisis. He tried his best to use his reputation and credibility in the industry to persuade 72 creditors in Beijing to jointly petition the Ministry of Justice to suspend the execution of the bankruptcy. Meanwhile, he sent people to the branches nationwide to clean up the accounts. After eight years of cleaning up and rectification, Rishengchang resumed business in 1922, but it never regained its former glory. After struggling to stay in business for ten years, it finally ceased its century-old banking business.

Out of the virtue of saving people in danger, Liang Huaiwen, who could have stayed away from the whole thing, saved the tottering Rishengchang. He kept the promise he made to the owner when he started to serve as the manager and kept the honor and reputation of Rishengchang.

> **ZHOU JIANBO**
> **DIRECTOR OF DEPARTMENT OF ECONOMIC HISTORY,**
> **SCHOOL OF ECONOMICS, PEKING UNIVERSITY**
> **VICE PRESIDENT OF CHINA SOCIETY FOR THE HISTORY OF**
> **ECONOMIC THOUGHTS**
>
> "Piaohao" held unlimited liability, and modern banks are limited companies. Because of that, many "piaohao" and Shanxi merchants' stores, represented by Rishengchang, collapsed after one single branch failed. The forms used in "piaohao" are different from those in modern banks. During crises such as war and unrest, the advantages and disadvantages of the industry would be fully shown.

At the beginning of the 20th century, the warlords threw the country into chaos, and the people lived in misery. The operation of the private banks set up by Shanxi merchants was affected. There used to be more than 500 private banks all around the country. After the Revolution of 1911, this number was reduced to less than 40 in 1917. At this point, if Shanxi merchants could give up the principle of making only ethical profit, they could definitely take advantage of the chaos to make a fortune and turn the table. However, in this life-and-death situation, they almost collectively chose to sacrifice their livelihood for righteousness.

In the 1930s, the Jin banknotes issued by Shanxi Provincial Bank were devalued due to the loss of the Central Plains War. In order to reverse the financial chaos, the reorganized Shanxi Provincial Bank issued the exchange voucher, also known as the new banknote, and offered to buy back Jin banknotes at the ratio of 1:25. At that time, many private banks set up by Shanxi merchants had the business of depositing and loaning Jin banknotes. If the depositors were paid in Jin notes, their deposits would be devalued, and the private banks could make a fortune. But they didn't benefit themselves at the expense of others. Instead, they paid depositors who deposited Jin banknote in the new banknote. In this way, the depositors' deposits retained their value, while the private banks suffered losses.

"I'd rather lose all my money than let the customers lose theirs. " To maintain their reputation, most private banks chose to take the loss from the devaluation of Jin banknote themselves, which caused the deficit to keep growing and finally break them down.

Under the setting sun, the glorious legend of Piaohao, or private banks, was eventually locked in the past. But the light of Shanxi merchants' philosophy of righteousness and integrity still shines brightly as ever through the closed door.

重然诺、守诚信、讲义气，这是晋商驰骋商界的独家秘笈。没有信用，就没有立足之地；没有信义，就没有立世之本。面对商海利益的诱惑，"以诚争取机会，以信把握机会"一直是晋商景行行止的道德品质。他们坚信"天道"也"酬信"，付出诚信，就一定能收获利益、聚集财富。"言而有信、行为有诚、心中有敬"，最终成就了晋商商行天下的繁荣。

时空流转，曾经的财富帝国早已烟消云散，但"讲仁爱、重民本、守诚信、崇正义、尚和合、求大同"这些代表着中华优秀传统文化的价值理念，随着晋商故事的广为流传，被具象化为这一群体的写意素描，被感知、被接受、被弘扬，并传承至今。

纪录片《寻踪晋商》第三集：
《以义制利的独家秘诀》

Valuing integrity and righteousness was Shanxi merchants' secret to succeed in the business world. Without integrity, one couldn't gain a foothold in the world, not to mention develop a business. Facing the temptation of interests, Shanxi merchants always adhered to the belief of striving for opportunities with sincerity and grasping opportunities with integrity. They believed that integrity would always be rewarded and that integrity was the key to making profit and accumulating wealth. And such philosophy eventually achieved Shanxi merchants' magnificent business legend in the world.

As time goes by, the empire of wealth has long since disappeared. But the ideas representing the excellent traditional Chinese culture, including valuing benevolence, people, integrity, justice, harmony, and unity, have spread with the stories of Shanxi merchants. They have become the labels of this group, being perceived, accepted, carried forward, and passed down to this day.

第四章　传奇商帮的商业伦理

Business Ethics of the Legendary Merchant Group

Part 4

和衷共济、和合共生是中华民族的历史基因，也是东方文明的精髓。从相与间的扶持，到商帮间的携手，再到跨国界的合作，扬鞭万里的山西商人，把和衷共济的商业伦理播撒在他们驰骋过的每一片土地上。

Harmony and symbiosis are the historical genes of the Chinese nation and the essence of oriental civilization. From mutual support, to the cooperation between businessmen, and then to cross-border cooperation, Shanxi businessmen have sown the business ethics of harmony in every piece of land they gallop through.

"不到园林，怎知春色如许。"诞生于江苏昆山的昆曲，在江南的氤氲水汽和檀板笙箫中浸润百年，柔软、细腻、婉约。

然而，中国唯一的昆曲博物馆，却是粗犷豪放的北方商人当年在异乡兴建的晋商会馆。

300多年前，山西商人走到哪儿，就把会馆建到哪儿。晋北的莜面窝窝和江南的水晶粉糯米圆子在这里烩成佳肴；梆子戏的高门大嗓和昆山腔的浅吟低唱在这里回响交流；山西人的北方官话与江浙人的吴侬软语在这里热络攀谈……各种"和而不同"的元素就这样和谐共生、和衷共济，把中国老百姓日用而不觉的"和文化"演绎得淋漓尽致。

晋商会馆鼎盛时多达558处，几乎遍及全国所有的商都集镇和商埠码头，甚至远涉欧亚。

台上的戏，越唱越热闹；台下的人，越处越亲厚。从相与间的扶持，到商帮间的携手，再到跨国界的合作，扬鞭万里的山西商人，把和衷共济的商业伦理播撒在他们驰骋而过的每一片土地上。

How would you know the spring is this beautiful without going into the gardens?

However, this one and only Kunqu Opera Museum in China was originally a guild hall built by the bold Shanxi merchants.

Over 300 years ago, where there were Shanxi merchants, there would be their guild halls. The rolled hulless oats lasagna from northern Shanxi and the crystal glutinous rice balls of southern China were served together. The loud shouts of Bangzi Opera and the gentle whispers of Kunqu Opera mingled and echoed with each other. Both Shanxi people's northern Mandarine and the soft dialect of Jiangsu and Zhejiang could often be heard in conversation. Various different elements coexisted in harmony and together promoted the development of the place, fully reflecting the Chinese culture of harmony that the people practiced every day without even realizing it.

In its heyday, there were as many as 558 Shanxi merchant guild halls, covering almost all of the country's commercial towns and ports, and even parts of Europe and other Asian countries.

As the performance on stage got better and better, the people watching it became closer and closer. From mutual assistance between individuals to collaboration between merchant groups, then to international cooperation, Shanxi merchants spread their business philosophy of joining hands to achieve common prosperity on every piece of land they galloped through.

赊店古镇山陕会馆
Shanshan Guild Hall in ancient town on credit

壹

在河南南阳，潘河与赵河结伴而行，穿过赊店古镇 1900 年的历史。"白天千帆过，夜晚万盏灯"，明清时期，这里是驰名全国的水陆码头，也是万里茶道的中转站。

一座赊店镇，半部商业史。200 多年前，在这座山陕两省商人合资搭建的戏台上，生旦净末丑，唱尽人间百态、世事春秋。很难想象，这热热闹闹的一出好戏，竟会是一项惩罚制度。

当年山西商人在外乡建造会馆时，往往要把戏台搭在关公大殿的正对面。一旦有谁违反了行规，就罚他掏钱请戏班唱戏，向关老爷赔罪。

清朝雍正年间，在赊店的商贸市场上，出现了不少用"大秤进小秤出"的手段缺斤短两、暗中牟利的不法商人，以至于老百姓到集市上买东西，都要自己带上一杆秤。为了杜绝欺诈行为、维护市场公平，山陕两省商人齐聚会馆商定对策。而他们的办法，就是制定行规，统一大小秤的度量衡标准。如果有谁不用这种标准秤，那就"罚戏三场"。

一项充满人性和温情的惩罚制度，被刻在了冰冷的石碑上。是仪式，更是一种宣示：制度如磐石，坚不可废！

公元1724年刻立的《同行商贾公议戥秤定规概碑》，被认为是"中国最早的工商管理法规"。虽然只有短短几行字，却把一直以来靠德行和自律维系的市场秩序，第一次变成了明确的规则文字。其实，在当时，距离法国人颁布世界上第一部商法典，还要再等80多年时间。"商法"仍是一个尚未诞生的名词，所以到底何为"不法"，谁也无从界定，更无权惩戒。

中国人民大学西班牙籍教授　哈维尔·加西亚

第一个类似行会的组织于1901年在伦敦成立，后来在1931年，国际标准诞生，行会演变成了商会，他们为产品和质量标准制定了规则。在我看来，晋商类似行会的组织应该先于或者同步于欧洲，早在18世纪末19世纪初就开始了。

在国际经济合作中，正常的贸易关系是建立在等价交换基础上的互惠互利，而不是你多我少、你输我赢的"零和博弈"。

山西大学晋商学研究所副所长　刘成虎

公平交易、互惠互利已成为国内外的交易者所共同追求的国际理念或者国际规则。但是在中国封建社会，商法商律是缺失的，政府对经济、对市场的管理又相对松散。在这样的一种环境下，山西商人为了更好地维护市场交易主体的利益，就成立了会馆，组成了所谓的商业组织，共同维护商业秩序。山陕会馆就是山西商人和陕西商人在异地共同组建而形成的一种联合体。

在赊店山陕会馆现存的九块碑刻中，有七块记述了当年山陕商人共同制定的商业道德规则。立于清乾隆五十年的《公议杂货行规碑》，刻录的商业行规更是多达18项。

河南省南阳市社旗县赊店商埠文化产业示范区
管委会副主任　赵静

这块石碑的内容涉及面非常广，比如说不能私自设立招牌、不能强买强卖、不能打价格战等等，这些其实是当时秦晋两地商人共同商议的一种行业规则。所以说，山陕会馆不仅是一个通商情、崇忠义的地方，更是一个行业的自律机构。正是有了这种自律，商人们才形成了巨大的合力，才促成了当时的商贸迅速发展。

商代青铜器"鸮卣"　山西博物院
Xiaoyou, a Bronze Wine Vessel from the Shang Dynasty
Shanxi Museum

　　和衷共济、和合共生是中华民族的历史基因，也是东方文明的精髓，和而更强，合而更远。

　　在山西博物院有一个来自数千年前的精灵叫"鸮卣"，是两只呆萌的猫头鹰背靠背紧紧相依。上面的盖子与下面的器皿贴合在一起，像极了古汉语中的"合"字。它仿佛是一个精神图腾，完美地诠释着中华文明包容差异、和谐共进的深刻智慧。

　　世界因"和"而存在，因"合"而发展，200多年前的山西商人早已深谙此理。而今天，面对共建人类命运共同体的全球使命，面对"零和博弈还是合作共赢"的时代之问，中国人再一次坚定作答：走共商共建共享之路，共同做大人类社会现代化的"蛋糕"。而这份坚定，正是源自民族基因中"和为贵"的文化自觉。

同行商贾公议戥秤定规概碑

赊旗店，四方商客集货兴贩之墟。原初码头买卖行户原有数家，年来人烟稠多，开张卖载者二十余家。其间即有改换戥称大小不一独网其利，内弊难除。是以，同行商贾会同集头等齐集关帝庙，公议称足十六两，戥依天平为则，庶乎较准均匀者，公平无私，俱各遵依。同行有和气之雅，宾主无疎庋之情，公议之后不得暗私戥称之更换，犯此者罚戏三台，如不遵者举秤禀官究治，惟恐日后紊乱规则，同众禀明县主蔡老爷，金批钧谕，永除大弊。

山西平阳府□□□□□□□□□□□□□□□

集头：杨一朝　主持道人　舒功志　首人：（商号漫漶从略）　石匠　王首荣

萧成元　　　　　　　　　王首荣刊

大清雍正二年 菊月 重刻 行头 隆茂店 全立

大清同治元年九月初九日 大生店

1

In Nanyang, Henan Province, the Panhe River and the Zhaohe River run through the 1,900-year-old Shedian Ancient Town. "Thousands of boats pass by during the daytime, and tens of thousands of lights light up the night." During the Ming and Qing Dynasties, this town was a nationally renowned wharf and a transit station on the Tea Road.

Shedian Town itself represents half of the history of commerce. More than 200 years ago, operas that told wonderful stories of various eras were staged in this theater built by Shanxi and Shaanxi merchants.

But those lively scenes were actually the result of a penalty system.

During the reign of Emperor Yongzheng in the Qing Dynasty, some unscrupulous merchants appeared, who made improper profits by using two different sets of scales. As a result, some people chose to take their own scales when making purchases at the market.

Shanxi and Shaanxi merchants gathered in the guild hall to find a way to prevent fraud and maintain market fairness. They eventually decided to establish a set of rules and standardized the weights and measures of the scales. Those who refused to follow the standard would be punished by treating the others to three opera performances.

A punishment system giving out the warmth of humanity was engraved on the cold hard stone tablet. It was a ceremony, and it was more like a declaration that the system was as unbreakable as stones.

This Tablet of the Agreed Standard of Dengzi Scales by Peer Merchants carved in 1724 is considered to be China's earliest business administration regulations. A few lines turned the market order, which was used to be maintained by virtue and self-discipline, into clear rules and regulations for the first time.

That period was more than 80 years before the French enacted the world's first commercial code. As the term commercial law was not created yet, no one could define what was legal and what was not, let alone punishment.

> **JAVIER GARCÍA, SPANISH PROFESSOR**
> **RENMIN UNIVERSITY OF CHINA**
> The first organization was established in London in 1901. Later, in 1931, international standards were born and formal guilds came into being. They established rules for products and quality standards. In my opinion, Shanxi merchants built their guild-like organizations earlier than or at the same time as Europe-as early as the 18th century

In international economic cooperation, normal trading relationships are mutually beneficial on the basis of equal exchange, rather than zero-sum games in which there is only one winner.

> **LIU CHENGHU, DEPUTY DIRECTOR**
> **INSTITUTE OF SHANXI MERCHANTS STUDIES, SHANXI UNIVERSITY**
> Nowadays, fair trade and mutual benefits have become a global consensus and rule. However, in China at that time, there were no commercial laws or regulations, and the government's management of the market and economy was relatively loose. In such an environment, in order to better protect the interests of the main body of the market transactions, Shanxi merchants formed business organizations and built guild halls, which served to maintain business order. The Shanxi-Shaanxi Guild Hall was an association that Shanxi

and Shaanxi merchants together formed in places away from their hometowns.

Among the surviving nine tablets in the Shanxi-Shaanxi Guild Hall in Shedian Town, seven record the rules of business ethics that were jointly formulated by Shanxi and Shaanxi merchants at that time. The Tablet of Agreed Rules for Grocery Stores carved in 1785 recorded as many as 18 business rules.

ZHAO JING
DEPUTY DIRECTOR, MANAGEMENT COMMITTEE OF INDUSTRIAL DEMONSTRATION ZONE OF SHEDIAN BUSINESS CULTURE, SHEQI COUNTY, HENAN PROVINCE

The content of this tablet covers a very wide range of issues, such as the prohibition of private signboards, the prohibition of hard sell, and the prohibition of price wars, which were actually the industry rules formulated by Shanxi and Shaanxi merchants at that time. That is to say, the Shanxi-Shaanxi Guild Hall was not just a place where people exchanged information and made friends. It was also a self-regulatory organization, which enabled the merchants to make joint efforts and achieved the rapid development of trade and commerce at that time.

Harmony and unity are in the genes of the Chinese nation. They are the essence of the Eastern civilization. Harmony and unity lead to strength and a brighter future.

This elf from thousands of years ago is called Xiaoyou, which looks like two cute owls clinging to each other back to back. The lid and the vessel are fitted together, resembling the ancient Chinese character of He, meaning unity. It is the spiritual totem of the Shanxi people, which perfectly illustrates the profound wisdom of Chinese civilization to tolerate differences and work together in harmony.

The world exists because of harmony and grows because of unity. Shanxi merchants already understood this more than 200 years ago. Today, the world faces a global mission of building a community with a shared future for mankind and a choice between zero-sum games and win-win cooperation. Chinese people are once again determined to make joint efforts and make the pie of humanity's modernization bigger. This solid faith comes from the culture of harmony that flows in the veins of Chinese people.

制作千两茶
Make a thousand teas

贰

"伙计们，加把子劲，重些压杠，慢些滚茶……"，在湖南安化，男人们的"踩茶号子"已唱了两百多年。一支粗大壮硕的千两黑茶，在七八个壮汉雄浑粗犷的号子声中诞生了。

根据不同的制作工艺和发酵程度，中国人把茶分为绿茶、白茶、黄茶、青茶、红茶和黑茶，而安化，是黑茶的故乡。

200多年前，在黑茶飘香的季节，一位山西茶商马掌柜与安化茶商谌冠英在资江相遇。当时，马掌柜乘坐的木船触礁进水，刚好碰到了回乡探亲的谌冠英，于是便搭船同行。当谌冠英的船驶入安化和桃江的交接处时，突然出现了一帮劫匪，当

晋丰厚
Jin Fengfeng

时马掌柜身上还带有一大包银子。

湖南安化晋丰厚茶行第七代传人　谌超美

对，没错，当时这种情形下，我们家这位老爷爷急中生智，用船篷做掩护，把银子就藏到了芦苇荡中。劫匪上了船之后没有搜到任何有价值的东西，只能扫兴而回，我们家老爷爷返回芦苇荡，把马掌柜的银子又拿出来，保全了马掌柜的财产。

事后谌冠英才知道，这位姓马的山西客人，是榆次常家的大掌柜，来安化采办茶叶。巧的是，谌氏一脉正是安化的制茶世家。两人一路相谈甚欢，竟促成了万里茶道上一段跨越晋湘两省的合作。公元1810年，山西榆次常家和湖南安化谌家携手创办"晋丰厚"商号。谌家人还把一

千两茶

A surname

些北方民居特有的木雕窗棂和高高门槛,搬到了自家的宅院里。他们用这样的方式怀念那段200多年前的晋湘情缘。

其实山西商人与安化茶商的渊源,远不止常谌两家。湖南安化黑茶博物馆里,一本200多年前的《行商遗要》,记载着当年资江上"茶市斯为最,人烟两岸稠"的繁荣景象。特别是至今传颂晋湘两省的"千两茶"的故事。安化盛产竹子。当年山西商人一路贩茶,发现了这一点。他们利用竹片编成篾篓,制成紧压茶。既节省了空间,又能防止茶叶走味变质。这些茶被称为"千两茶",号称"世界茶王",每卷茶以老秤计算是1000两,也就是现在的36.25公斤。千两茶其实不止千两。由于陆路运输会因气候干燥导致茶叶缩水,于是茶商在包装压制时多压进去一二百两,以确保运达目的地后千两茶是足额甚至超额的。

《行商遗要》
Relics of Merchants

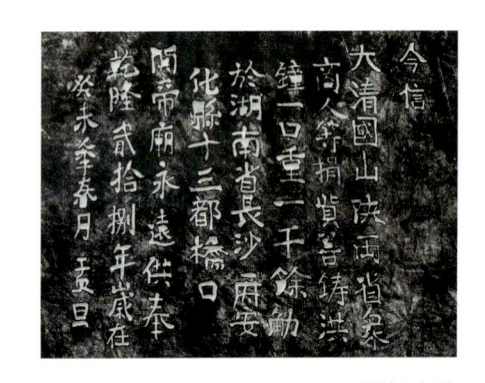

茶钟及拓片
Tea bell and rubbing

中国黑茶博物馆馆长　宁中

当时安化有句谚语"茶是草，客是宝，茶客不来不得了"。讲的是安化有很多人，一年到头都是以茶叶为生。如果山西客人不过来，他们的茶叶卖不掉，这一年的生计就没有着落。

安化永锡桥
Anhua Yong Tin Bridge

清代，在资江边开茶行的山西商号多达 300 余家。永锡桥的碑刻上，写下他们捐资建桥的慷慨故事；黑茶博物馆里，矗立着山陕商人共同捐铸的茶钟；漫漫茶路上，那些跨山越海的患难深情、和衷共济的珍贵记忆，也被晋商子孙镌刻在深宅大院中富有南方气质的台轩阁榭里。

常家第十八代后人　常欣

这个就是典型的南方砖雕，小狮子的表情调皮可爱，和北方庄重威严的狮子的表情在风格上有很大的差别。现在我们看到的庄园里面有一些砖雕，都是当年常家从扬州带回来的工匠，用江浙一带的紫金泥，先雕再烧，最后成型。而且当时常家庄园里种植了大量的南方植物，形成了一座典型的南北文化融合的园林。

常家庄园小狮子砖雕
Small lion brick carving in Chang Jia Manor

　　一草一木、一砖一瓦，这些婉约秀气的南方来客，似乎并没有对黄土高原水土不服，它们把根深深扎在这片土地上，融进一座座晋商大院之中。

2

"Come on, guys. Press the bar hard and roll the tea slowly." In Anhua, Hunan Province, men have been singing this song of tea-making for over 200 years. A thick stick of dark tea was just made in the unconstrained songs of several strong men.

According to different production processes and degrees of fermentation, Chinese people classify tea into green tea, white tea, yellow tea, oolong tea, black tea, and dark tea, and Anhua is the hometown of dark tea.

Over 200 years ago, in the season of dark tea, a tea merchant from Shanxi met Shen Guanying, a tea merchant from Anhua, on the Zijiang River.

This is the Zijiang River, a tributary of the Yangtze River. It's among the major four rivers in Hunan. In history, it was the golden channel used to transport the dark tea of Anhua to other places. More than 200 years ago, Manager Ma, who worked for the Chang family of Shanxi, came to Anhua to purchase tea. When he got here, the wooden boat he was in hit a reef and leaked. Shen Guanying, an ancestor of the Shen family, was on his way home and happened to pass by, then the two took the same boat.

It's said that when Shen Guanying's boat reached the junction of Anhua and Taojiang, a gang of robbers suddenly appeared, and Manager Ma had a large bag of silver with him at that time.

That's right. In that situation, Shen Guanying thought on his feet and hid the silver in the reeds using the boat canopy as a cover. The robbers found nothing valuable on the boat and left in frustration. Later, Shen Guanying and Manager Ma returned to the reeds and retrieved Manager Ma's silver, preserving his property.

Later, Shen Guanying came to know that this guest surnamed Ma from Shanxi was the manager working for the Chang family in Yuci, who went to Anhua to purchase tea. Coincidentally, the Shen family happened to be a renowned tea-making family in Anhua. The two had a great time, which resulted in the two families' cooperation spanning Shanxi and Hunan along the Tea Road. In 1810, the Chang family in Yuci, Shanxi Province and the Shen family in Anhua, Hunan Province jointly established the trade name Jinrich Tea.

The wooden window lattices with carved patterns and high thresholds, which were characteristic of northern residences, were moved by the Shen family to their houses in the south. In this way, they commemorated the friendship spanning Shanxi and Hunan more than 200 years ago and the story of the Thousand-Tael Tea, which is still being told in the two provinces.

I've found that Anhua is abundant in bamboo. Back then, Shanxi merchants also realized it when traveling along the Tea Road. They weaved baskets with bamboo strips and made compacted tea, which allowed them to save space as well as prevent the tea from going bad.

This is the Thousand-Tael Tea pressed by bamboo strips, which is also known as the king of tea. Each tea stick weighs 1,000 taels, equivalent to about 36.25 kilograms today.

The Thousand-Tael Tea actually weighed more than 1,000 taels. During land transportation, the dry climate would cause tea to shrink, so the tea traders always put an extra 100 to 200 tales of tea in the packaging to ensure that the delivered tea could weigh at least 1,000 taels.

There are so many more stories between Shanxi merchants and Anhua tea traders other than that of the Chang and Shen families. In the Dark Tea Museum in Anhua, Hunan, this Business Summary from over 200 years ago recorded the scenes of the prosperous tea market along the Zijiang River.

NING ZHONG, CURATOR
CHINA DARK TEA MUSEUM
There was a proverb in Anhua that tea is a plant, customers are precious, and the customers who buy tea are whom we count on. At that time, many people in Anhua made a living by making and selling tea. Without the customers from Shanxi, their tea wouldn't sell, and their livelihood would become a problem.

In the Qing Dynasty, there were more than 300 Shanxi merchants who opened tea stores along the Zijiang River. The inscriptions on Yongxi Bridge tell the story of them making donations to build the bridge. In the Dark Tea Museum stands the tea bell donated by Shanxi and Shaanxi merchants. The precious memories of mutual help and joint efforts on the long Tea Road have also been engraved by the descendants of Shanxi merchants in the pavilions and terraces with southern characteristics.

CHANG XIN
EIGHTEENTH-GENERATION DESCENDANT OF THE
CHANG FAMILY
This is a brick carving typical of southern China. You can see the little lion is cute and adorable, which is completely different from the solemn and majestic stone lions in the north.
The brick carvings we see now were made by the craftsmen that the Chang family brought back from Yangzhou. With the purple-gold clay from Jiangsu

and Zhejiang, they carved, burned, and shaped their works. Coupled with a large number of plants from southern China that were planted in the Chang family's manor, they formed a typical garden where the northern and southern cultures were fused.

Grass, trees, bricks, tiles and other graceful elements from the south seemed to have no trouble fitting into the Loess Plateau at all. They took root in this land.

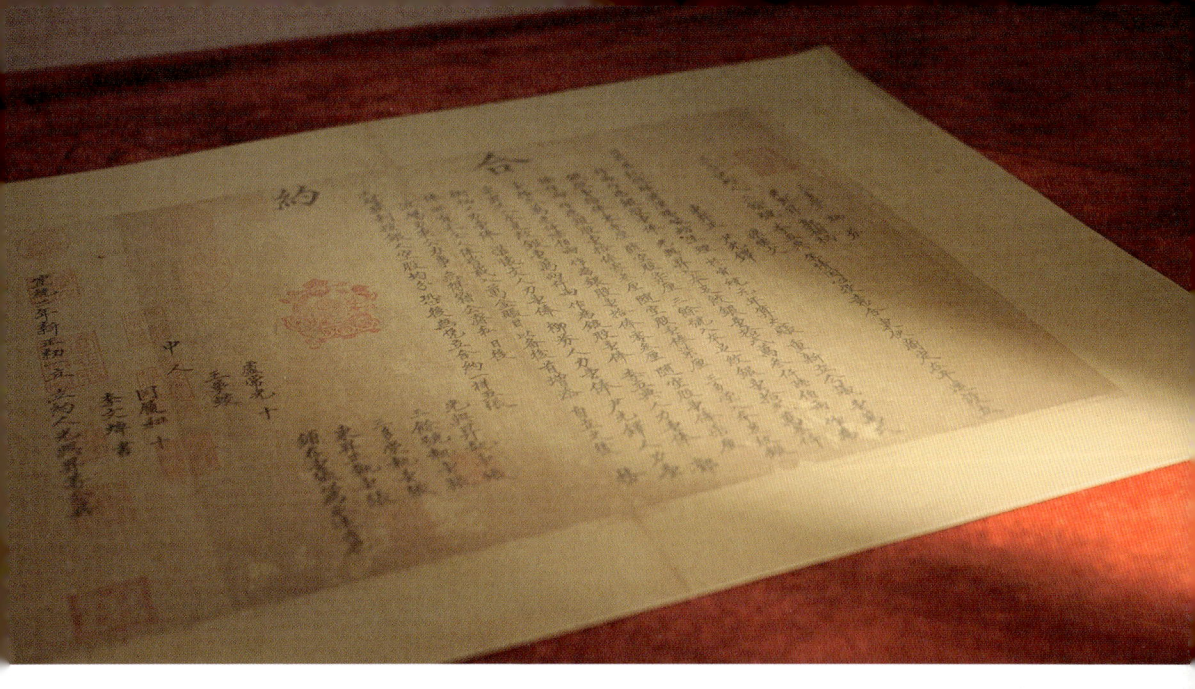

日昇昌票号合约（1910 年）
Nisheng Chang Ticket Number Contract (1910)

叁

"东家财股，二十一股。本账期同仁身股分红，十七股。一股平均为一万五千八百一十六两五。天津刘寿熹老帮，七厘……"算盘一响，白银万两。在晋商票号三年一次的股东分红大会上，全场最高股拿到了一万五千两分红。而在当时的中国，一个县官的年薪，也不过千余两。

19 世纪 20 年代到 20 世纪初，全国 50% 以上的金融机构都挤在平遥古城中一条不足八百米的街道上，也是在这里，诞生了中国票号业最早的股份合作制。

山西商人早在创设票号之初就发现，开办一家票号所需的巨额资金，即便是把几代人的家业都搭进去也远远不够。如果能把分散在相与同行间的财富聚拢起来，形成一种利益绑定的协作机制，那么不仅可以解决资金的燃眉之急，还能实现可持续的共赢，银股由此而生。

上海财经大学讲席教授
山西财经大学晋商研究院学术院长　燕红忠

"银股"，就是财力股，是财东出资通过资本来分红的一种形式。每家票号股东，多的时候 20 多个，少说也有 10 多个人，他们每人出资少则几千两，多则几万两甚至几十万两，这样众多出资人就坐在了一条船上，他们同舟共济、共谋发展。

在晋商票号的股份机制中，除了"银股"❶，还有一种"身股"❷。清末学者徐珂在《清稗类钞》中这样记述："出资者为银股，出力者为身股。"票号员工一旦拥有了"身股"，就相当于成为企业的合伙人，一荣俱荣、一损俱损。

马荀，是当年祁县乔家"复盛西"商号一个下属小粮店的业务员。从 4 年学徒到 10 年伙计，他几乎包揽了粮店八成以上的生意。有了这个超级业务员，粮店经营有方、连年盈利，甚至"复盛西"总号还时不时要靠小粮店来贴补亏空。然而，当年的马荀即便是少有的商

❶ 银股：又称财股。指的是东家出具资本后所占据的股份。通常一家票号会由若干个东家组成，拥有"银股"者是票号的所有者，也就是所谓的东家，他们决定大掌柜的任用和去留，承担经营的全部风险，并参与分红。

❷ 身股：又称"劳股"或"人力股"。这种股不用出钱，由东家根据员工的工龄、职务、贡献、工作态度等给予一定的股份。通常一股分为 10 厘，当员工工作一定年限，薪金达到 70 两银子时就可以开始享有"身股"，最低从厘开始（也有个别票号从零点几厘开始），最高可达到 10 厘（个别也有高于 10 厘的）。身股制度这一"中国式股权激励"，有利于建立起一个完整的人才遴选、培养、挽留机制。

界才俊，也只能领到区区 20 两白银的年薪。但票号掌柜除了上千两的年薪外，还享有 3 年一次上万两的分红。踌躇满志的马荀，向东家乔致庸提出辞职。

山西省晋商文化研究会会长　二级教授　刘建生

当时各家票号商号都存在这样的问题：各商家享受"身股"分红的只是少数的掌柜和重要人员，而一般伙计和学徒，他们是无法享受的。这样就导致许多的学徒在出徒以后，纷纷辞职立号，自立门户，造成了人才的流失，对于企业的发展非常不利。

谁也不会想到，一封粮店小伙计发出的辞职信，会为一次意义深远的改革创举写下了传奇注脚。企业人才、眼前利润、长远发展，精明的山西商人把这一个个砝码放在天平上来回掂量。人，是最大的生产力。深谙此理的乔致庸，不想失去任何一个能为自己创造更多财富、更大可能的人才。于是乔致庸做了一个巨大的决定：凡是愿意跟他在字号里继续创业发展的，都会给他们一定的身股。

上海财经大学讲席教授

山西财经大学晋商研究院学术院长　燕红忠

这项改革的核心就是由高层享受身股扩大到普通员工，这是身股制度的进一步创新。不论职位和身份高低，一律按劳动进行分配，论

贡献取得报酬。中国人崇尚"和为贵",而平等是合作的前提,也是和衷共济的一个基础。

"身股"制改革,很快就把票号伙计们的聪明才智充分调动起来,新开的分号一个接着一个,账上的利润一年一年翻番。在此后的10年中,乔东

平遥古城
The Ancient City of Ping Yao

家虽然把一半多的红利分给了伙计,但他的收益却是10年前的18.81倍。

晋商用身股制构建起一个员工与企业和衷共济的利益共同体,书写了中国历史上人力资源管理的一次创举。这项根本性变革释放出的巨大力量,也推动山西票号把商业触角伸向全球。一个"汇通天下"的黄金时代,扑面而来。

3 /

Owner holding, 21 shares. Staff holding, 17 shares. Each share averages 15, 816. 5 taels. Tianjin Manager Liu Shouxi. I get 0. 7 share. You can count it yourself.

The sound of the abacus always comes with thousands of taels of silver. This is the shareholders' meeting of the Shanxi merchants and it was held every three years. The largest shareholder got a dividend of 15, 000 taels of silver, while a county magistrate at that time could only make about 1, 000 taels of silver each year.

Between the 1820s and the early 1900s, more than 50% of the country's financial institutions were located on this street of less than 800 meters, and this was also the birthplace of the earliest form of joint-stock system in China's banking industry.

When setting up the first private banks, Shanxi merchants already realized that even the accumulated wealth of a family over generations couldn't cover the huge amount of capital required to start a private bank. But if they could gather together the wealth scattered among peers and form a collaborative system of binding interest, they would be able to solve the problem of funds as well as achieve a sustainable win-win situation. The joint-stock system was then formed.

YAN HONGZHONG
CHAIR PROFESSOR AT SHANGHAI UNIVERSITY OF FINANCE AND ECONOMICS
ACADEMIC DEAN OF INSTITUTE OF SHANXI MERCHANT STUDIES, SHANXI UNIVERSITY OF FINANCE AND ECONOMICS

> Financial shares were acquired by investing funds. A private bank would have around 10 to 20 shareholders, each of whom would make an investment of thousands of taels to hundreds of thousands of taels of silver. This way, the investors would have common interests and work together to make the business grow.

In the shareholding mechanism established by Shanxi merchants, except for financial shares, there were also labor shares. Xu Ke, a scholar in the late Qing dynasty, wrote in the Qing Petty Matters Anthology, that those who offered funds would have financial shares, and those who offered labor would have labor shares. Those who had labor shares would also be considered partners of the enterprise, and they would thus share a common destiny with the enterprise.

Ma Xun was a salesman at a grain store under Fushengxi, which belonged to the Qiao family in Qixian County. During his four years as an apprentice and ten years as a clerk, he closed almost 80% of the store's deals. With this super salesman, the store could make a profit every year, and even the main store of Fushengxi sometimes relied on that store to cover the deficit.

Though Ma Xun was a rarely seen business talent, his annual salary was only 20 taels of silver. The store manager, on the other hand, could make over 1,000 taels of silver every year and receive a dividend of tens of thousands of taels once every three years. As a result, the ambitious Ma Xun tendered his resignation.

No one expected that a clerk's resignation would make a legendary footnote for a far-reaching reform. Thinking about the talents of the enterprise, immediate profits, and long-term development, the shrewd Shanxi merchants weighed every weight over and over again.

> **LIU JIANSHENG, PRESIDENT**
> **SHANXI MERCHANTS CULTURE RESEARCH**
> **ASSOCIATION OF SHANXI PROVINCE**
> Ma Xun made the decision to quit and Qiao Zhiyong came to another important conclusion: those who were willing to continue to work for him would also receive shares in the business.

People are always the greatest productive force. Qiao Zhiyong, who was well aware of it, didn't want to lose any talent that could create more wealth and greater possibilities for him.

> **YAN HONGZHONG**
> **CHAIR PROFESSOR AT SHANGHAI UNIVERSITY OF**
> **FINANCE AND ECONOMICS**
> **ACADEMIC DEAN OF INSTITUTE OF SHANXI**
> **MERCHANTS STUDIES, SHANXI UNIVERSITY OF**
> **FINANCE AND ECONOMICS**
> The core of the reform was to allow ordinary employees to hold labor shares and receive dividends just like the executives, which was an innovation in the system of labor shares. Regardless of the status and position, everyone could get paid properly based on their contribution. Chinese people value harmony, and equality is the prerequisite and basis of sincere cooperation.

The reform of the labor share system soon got the employees fully motivated, allowing Qiao Zhiyong to make more and more money and open new branches one after another. In the following decade, although he gave more than half of the profits to his employees, his income was 18. 81 times that of 10 years ago.

Shanxi merchants established a community of common interest for employees and enterprises, accomplishing a pioneering feat in the history of human resource management in China. The tremendous power released by this fundamental change also enabled Shanxi merchants to extend their business to other parts of the world.

A golden era of conducting business throughout the world began.

太谷三多堂
Taigu Sanduotang

肆

福、禄、寿、禧、财，在中国文化中被称为"五福"。一句"五福临门"，是中国人对幸福人生最圆满的祈盼。

从空中俯瞰，这个"寿"字形的建筑，由三座院落套叠而成，所以得名"三多堂"，寓意多子、多福、多寿。当年太谷曹家兴建了"福""禄""寿""禧"四座大院，唯有这一座留存至今。不过，仅仅一座"三多堂"，便足以窥见当年的曹家曾创下一份多么富庶的家业。

中国商业史学会会长　王茹芹

道光咸丰年间，曹家商号已经遍及了半个中国，在国外也发展到了莫斯科，但是他们的主要阵地还是在东北。在当时东北的市场上，曹家、渠家、乔家，三家的地盘争斗战非常激烈。

"钱帖子"是一种原始纸币。在"钱帖子"上注明银两的数量和金额，就可以代替现金流通支付。清光绪年间，各家票号为方便客户不用随身携带大量现银，纷纷发行"钱帖子"。可一些别有用心之人，却惦记上了发行量较大的渠、乔两大商贾。

谣言跑得飞快，当渠、乔两家"钱帖子"要贬值的消息传遍全国，各地客商纷纷挤进票号，拿出手中的"钱帖子"兑换现银。四面八方涌来的挤兑潮，像一个接一个的巨浪，即便是财大气粗的晋商富贾，也被打得喘

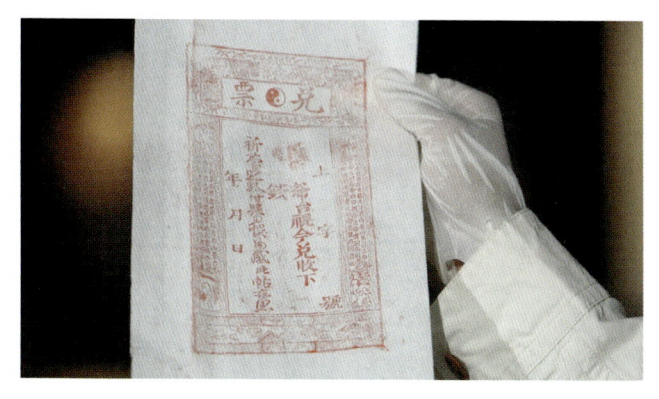

钱帖子
Paper money

不过气、翻不了身。渠、乔两家倾囊而出，但东北和内蒙古的票号，还是接连倒闭了。渠、乔两位大东家不得不硬着头皮向老对手曹家上门求援。

是竞争，还是竞合？是取利，还是重义？是趁人之危，还是慷慨相助？十几年的博弈赢局已定，可曹家却在最后一刻向对手伸出了援手，公开宣布曹家各地的票号均可代替乔、渠两家兑付现银。消息一出，挤兑风潮很快平息下来。

> **中国商业史学会会长　王茹芹**
> 当遇到市场危机时，乔、梁、曹三家联手救市，曹家以它的商誉、实力，挽救了两家企业生存的危机。晋商在市场风险中，在处理风险事件上，坚守和为贵、和衷共济，这个品质十分宝贵。

最后一刻举义救市的决定，存续了渠、乔两家的商脉，在东北市场，渠、乔两家处处谦让曹家，也使曹家的市场占有率进一步扩张。他们，从原来的竞争对手变成了商业伙伴。

逐利是商人的本性，可山西商人却常说："万两银子，不过一句话。"对商业伦理的坚守，自然会营造出健康的商业生态和营商环境。山西商人明白一个道理，"和衷"方能"共济"，要想基业长青，"共赢"应该成为大家共同遵守的行业规则和始终追求的商业理想。和气生财、和衷共济的商业伦理，也熔铸成他们一步步走向"海内最富"的核心竞争力。

4

Good fortune, emolument, longevity, happiness, and wealth are the five blessings in traditional Chinese culture. The phrase Five blessings come to your door represents the Chinese people's wish for a happy life.

From the air, this building complex with the shape of the Chinese character longevity has three courtyards. Therefore, it was named the Hall of Triple Abundance, meaning many children, good fortune, and longevity. The Cao family in Taigu at that time built four courtyards named fortune, emolument, longevity, and happiness respectively. This is the only one that remains today, which is already enough to show how wealthy the Cao family was in those years.

> **WANG RUQIN, PRESIDENT**
> **SOCIETY OF CHINESE COMMERCE HISTORY**
> During the reign of Emperor Daoguang and Emperor Xianfeng in the Qing Dynasty, the Cao family's stores branched in half of China, even reaching abroad in Moscow. But their main position was still in Northeast China, where the turf war between the Cao family, the Qu family, and the Qiao family was fierce.

This piece of paper, known as Qiantiezi, is a primitive type of paper money. When a certain amount of silver is written on it, it can be used as a substitute for cash in circulation. During the reign of Emperor Guangxu in the Qing Dynasty, many private banks issued their own paper money to help customers save the trouble of carrying around a large amount of silver. But some with evil motives targeted the Qu and Qiao families who issued a large number of paper money.

Rumors were flying that the paper money issued by the Qu and Qiao families were about to depreciate, causing their customers throughout the country to crowd into the branches to exchange the paper money into silver. The bank run was so severe that even such wealthy business families couldn't withstand it. The Qu and Qiao families did everything they could, but their branches in Northeast China and Inner Mongolia still closed down one after another. They had no choice but to ask their old rival, the Cao family, for help.

To compete or to merge?Morality or profit?To hit the rivals when they were down or to lend them a helping hand?After more than a decade of rivalry and facing victory within grasp, the Cao family unexpectedly reached out to the rivals at the last minute, announcing that the paper money issued by the Qiao and Qu families could be exchanged into silver at the branches of the Cao family's private bank. The news soon settled the bank run.

> **WANG RUQIN, PRESIDENT**
> **SOCIETY OF CHINESE COMMERCE HISTORY**
> When encountering a market crisis, the three families joined hands to resolve the crisis. The Cao family used its reputation and strength to save two enterprises in an existential crisis. Shanxi merchants adhered to the principle of harmony , and that is a very precious feature.

The last-minute decision to offer help allowed the Qu and Qiao families to survive the crisis and continue their businesses. In return, the two families made many concessions in the market in Northeast China and allowed the Cao family to further increase its market share. They went from being competitors to business partners.

寻踪
晋商

Pursuing profit is the nature of businessmen, but Shanxi merchants always said that a promise was worth ten thousand taels of silver. Adherence to business ethics naturally created a healthy business ecology and business environment. Shanxi merchants understood the truth that only by working together could they get through difficulties and realize common prosperity. To build a long-lasting business, win-win must become the pursuit as well as rule for everyone. The philosophy of developing business on the basis of harmony allowed them to gradually become the country's wealthiest merchants.

伍

19世纪中后期的中国，到处笼罩着落日的斜阳。清王朝在内忧外患中日渐衰朽，已经无力护佑子民的财富、尊严，甚至生命。

《天津条约》《北京条约》和《中俄陆路通商章程》的签订以及太平天国运动的影响，使中俄贸易格局发生根本性改变。俄商到中国内地采购贩运茶叶，不仅畅行无阻，而且税金低廉，"恰克图通商日渐衰败，中国茶行字号诸多歇业，以致120家仅存10家，尚在似有如无之间"。到公元1868年，恰克图只剩下4家山西老号。不甘坐以待毙的山西商人，决定联合行动，来一次绝地反击。

晋商驼队
Jinshang camel caravan

公元 1867 年，山西商人程化鹏、余鹏云、孔广仇代表商界向清政府提出了重新经营"归化—库伦—恰克图商道"的建议，得到政府支持，同时还争取到了削减茶税和赴俄境内贸易的条件。一时间，曾因俄商挤压不得不退守归化的中国商人，纷纷重返恰克图。从张家口、从包头、从乌里雅苏台、从科布多……在归化通司商会的统一调动下，数以万计的骆驼满载货物，向俄罗斯进发。伊尔库茨克、赤塔、托博尔斯克、托木斯克、新西伯利亚、比斯克、奥伦堡、莫斯科、彼得堡……一夜之间，中国商人的店铺开遍了俄罗斯东部和西伯利亚各地。恢复经营的第一年中国商人向俄国输出茶叶 11 万担，到第三年，就翻倍增加到一年 20 万担。

中国商人联手打了一场漂亮的翻身仗，在当时外交羸弱、屡战屡败的中国，涌动起一股鼓舞人心的力量。然而，接下来他们要面对的，却是传统商业力量与先进技术革命之间一场体力悬殊的较量，是信息时代对农耕文明的碾压颠覆。

公元 1871 年，一条海底电缆横跨欧亚，从莫斯科铺到了上海，俄国商人率先告别了驮马驿道，跨入电信时代。行商的关键在于信息畅通，可农耕文明孕育的车马驿道，又怎么跑得过信息时代的电报通讯？此时，归化城的大盛魁商号向同行们分享了一个土办法：训练一批机灵又跑得飞快的信狗，让它们在归化总号与各分号间传递信息。

内蒙古茶叶之路研究会会长　作家　邓九刚

过去草原上狼很多，为了保护信狗，就在狗的护项圈上钉了狼牙钉。

总号的员工把信缝到护项圈的夹层里，狗三天三夜不吃不喝跑到分号，分号的员工见了信便明白马上就要开始复市了，于是赶快组织货源，大挣一笔。

"黄耳传信"，是大盛魁百年来立于不败之地的商业机密。但此刻，他们毫不犹豫地把机密变成了同行共享的机遇。

内蒙古茶叶之路研究会会长　作家　邓九刚

300年间大盛魁创造的商业奇迹，包括它和商业伙伴之间的守望相助，对于商业的发展，对于万里茶道商贸的流通，作出了不可磨灭的巨大贡献。

自然，即便是一条能跑出每小时70公里极限速度的极品信狗，也无法跑赢瞬息万里的电报传输。这场山西商人的信狗与俄国人的电报之间的比赛，这场驼队和火车轮船之间的竞跑，在清政府作壁上观和工业革命等诸多因素的催化之下终告失败。万里茶道，画上了一个悲壮的句号。然而，东方商人和衷共济、共御外辱的集体智慧，却在那个饱受内忧外辱的黑暗年代，如一道曙光乍现。

5

In the second half of the 19th century, China was on the verge of falling, just like the setting sun. The Qing Dynasty was decaying amidst internal and external crises and was no longer able to protect the wealth, dignity, and even the lives of its people.

The signing of the Treaty of Tianjin, the Convention of Peking, and the Sino-Russian Land Trade Regulations, as well as the influence of the Taiping Rebellion, led to a fundamental change in the pattern of Sino-Russian trade. Russian merchants had unhindered access to Chinese mainland to purchase tea, and they only had to pay very low taxes. "Trade with Kyakhta is declining. Many of the Chinese tea stores are now out of business, and only 10 of the 120 are still open. The industry is barely alive. " By 1868, there were only four stores ran by Shanxi merchants in Kyakhta.

Not willing to sit still and meet their doom, Shanxi merchants decided to join forces and fight back.

In 1867, Shanxi merchants Cheng Huapeng, Yu Pengyun, and Kong Guangqiu, on behalf of the business community, proposed to the Qing government to re-open the Guihua-Kulun-Kyakhta trade route, which was approved by the government. They also persuade the government to cut tea taxes and allow the merchants to go to Russia to conduct business. Chinese merchants, who once had to retreat to Guihua due to the pressure from Russian merchants, returned to Kyakhta in droves. Setting out from Zhangjiakou, Baotou, Uliastai, Kobdo, and deployed by the Guihua Chamber of Commerce, tens of thousands of camels loaded with goods left for Russia.

Overnight, Chinese merchants' stores spread throughout eastern Russia and various parts of Siberia.

In the first year, Chinese merchants exported 110, 000 picul of tea to Russia, and in the third year, it doubled to 200, 000.

Chinese merchants worked together and successfully turned the table, which was an inspiring story in the country at that time as China was weak in diplomacy and kept losing battles. However, what awaited them next was a lopsided battle between the traditional commercial forces and the advanced technological revolution, a crushing subversion of the agrarian civilization by the information age.

In 1871, a submarine cable was laid across Europe and Asia from Moscow to Shanghai, making Russian merchants the first to say goodbye to the horses and enter the age of telecommunications.

The key to running a successful business lies in the smooth flow of information, but how could the horses and carriages of the farming civilization outrun the telegraph of the information age? At this time, Dashengkui Firm in Guihua shared with its peers an old-fashioned method, to train some smart and fast-running mail dogs and let them pass messages between the headquarters in Guihua and the branches.

> **DENG JIUGANG, WRITER**
> **PRESIDENT OF INNER MONGOLIA TEA ROAD**
> **RESEARCH ASSOCIATION**
> The dogs would rush non-stop for three days and nights to deliver the messages. There used to be a lot of wolves on the prairie, so they would wear a collar with spikes for protection, and the letter would be kept in the interlayer of the collar. When the dogs returned, the merchants would know the latest trends in the market and get the goods ready.

Using dogs for communication was a trade secret that kept Dashengkui among the top firms for hundreds of years. At this point, it turned this secret into an opportunity for all its peers with no hesitation.

> **DENG JIUGANG, WRITER**
> **PRESIDENT OF INNER MONGOLIA TEA ROAD**
> **RESEARCH ASSOCIATION**
> The business miracle created by Dashengkui during the 300 years, including the mutual support between it and its business partners, played an indelible role in the development of commerce and the Tea Road.

Of course, even the best mail dogs that could run up to 70 kilometers per hour had no chance to beat the speed of the telegraph. This race between Shanxi merchants' mail dogs and Russian telegraph, and between camels and advanced vehicles, eventually ended with Chinese merchants' failure due to many factors such as the inaction of the Qing government and the Industrial Revolution. The Tea Road stretching for tens of thousands of kilometers ushered in its sad but noble ending. However, the collective wisdom of Chinese merchants to work together and fight against foreign bullies was like a ray of light in that dark era of internal and external crises.

青山遮不住，毕竟东流去。

虽然骆驼终究跑不赢火车，茶工的双手也赶不上机器的效率，但历史已经反复告诉人们，同处一个社会、一个地球，"和而不同""美美与共"，不但是人与人相处的根本道理，也是商业竞争中实现共赢的基本规则，更是全世界携手共建人类命运共同体的重要内涵。

坚持和衷共济的山西商人，不但创造了属于自己的商业辉煌，也为构建和谐文明的美好世界，提供了他们的价值探索。

纪录片《寻踪晋商》第四集：
《传奇商帮的商业伦理》

Blue mountains can't stop water flowing; Eastward the river keeps on going.

Although camels can never outrun the trains and the hands of tea workers are no match for machines, history has repeatedly told people that living in the same society and on the same planet, harmony in diversity is the fundamental premise for people to get along with each other, the basic rule to achieve win-win in commercial competition, and an important part of the vision of a community with a shared future for mankind.

Shanxi merchants, who stuck to the philosophy of joining hands to achieve common prosperity, wrote their glorious story of commerce. Moreover, they also did their part of exploration for the construction of a harmonious and civilized world.

第五章　家国天下的晋商风骨

The Patriotism of Shanxi Merchants

Part 5

"穷则独善其身，达则兼济天下"，明清晋商胸怀经世济民的天下情怀，扶危济困、兴办实业、捐资办学，在横贯亚欧大陆的商道上，晋商的经贸活动不仅促进经济社会发展，带动城市繁荣，也对商道沿线的文明交流互鉴起到了重要作用。

In difficult times, one focuses on self-cultivation;after achieving success, In the trade route across the Eurasian continent, the economic and trade activities of the Jin merchants not only promoted economic and social development and promoted the prosperity of the city, but also played an important role in the exchange and mutual learning of civilizations along the trade route.

对于"经济"一词的理解，古希腊哲学家亚里士多德认为，经济活动的目的是幸福，不是金钱。而幸福，是必须要通过参与公共服务，与他人建立起爱的关系。

隋朝著名思想家、教育家王通认为，"经济"就是经邦济世、经国济民。王通出生在晋商故里山西祁县，在他的著作《文中子·礼乐篇》中，第一次提出了"经济"一词："皆有经济之道，谓经国济民。"王通所倡导的"经国济民"的儒家思想，不仅影响了一代又一代中国人，而且滋养出了虽处财货之场，却修高明之行，谋利而不污的山西商人。他们用朴素的东方智慧，为亚里士多德的经济伦理写下深刻注脚。

As for the understanding of the word "jingji", the ancient Greek philosopher Aristotle believed that the purpose of economic activity is happiness, not money. Happiness is about having a loving relationship with others through participation in public services.

Wang Tong, a famous thinker and educator in the Sui Dynasty, believed that "jingji" was to help the world through the state and the country and the people. Wang Tong was born in Qixian County, Shanxi, the hometown of Shanxi merchants. He came up with the concept of "jingji" for the first time in his masterpiece Wenzhongzi, and believed it meant administering the state to relieve the suffering of the people. His concept of administering the state to relieve the suffering of the people influenced generations of Chinese people. It also cultivated the virtues of being upright and honest among Shanxi merchants. What they did with the wisdom of the East were profound footnotes to Aristotle's business ethics.

壹

诺贝尔经济学奖得主、剑桥大学教授奥格斯·丹顿(Angus Deaton)在关于贫富与幸福的研究中曾这样论述：这世界上的富有者每个人拿出一块美金，就能够使全世界的贫困者脱贫。看似多么简单的一件事，却是人类几千年文明史上一道未解的难题。因为富人未必都愿意拿出那一块钱，即便拿出来了，又怎样才能做到科学合理的分配呢？然而，这道未解之题，却有一份答案，被藏在140多年前的一座古戏楼里。

公元1877年，一场罕见的特大灾荒席卷中国北方。在这场被称为"230年未见之惨凄，未闻之悲痛"的"丁戊奇荒"❶中，山西、河南两省受灾最严重。史料记载：山西受灾达90多个州县，灾民有800多万。3年大灾，全省的人口损失高达48%。人畜大量死亡，致使商队运输无以为继，晋商对俄茶叶贸易只有寻常年份的4%，不仅生意惨淡，还得承担巨额违约赔偿。

大灾之年，度日维艰，在山西外贸世家常家发生了一件奇怪的事，一座规模并不大的戏楼，却有数万人次参与修建。当时常家养活全家800口人已非易事，却为何偏偏要在这个时候耗资修建戏楼呢？其实常家修戏楼，是为了给灾民们提供一种有尊严的以工代赈的接济。不管男女老少，只要每天搬一块砖，就管一天的饭。所以大灾持续了3年，常家的戏楼也整整修建了3年。

❶ 丁戊奇荒：中国华北地区发生于公元1875年至公元1878年之间的一场罕见的特大旱灾饥荒。1877年为丁丑年，1878年为戊寅年，因此史称"丁戊奇荒"。这场灾害波及山西、直隶、陕西、河南、山东等省，造成1000余万人饿死，另有2000余万灾民逃荒到外地，对中国晚清历史产生了深远影响。

常家戏楼
Chang home theatre

　　面对百年不遇的特大灾荒，平遥日昇昌票号掌柜邱泰基搭起粥棚，接济了数以万计的灾民；祁县乔东家乔致庸，不许全家老小做新衣、吃山珍，为灾民熬粥的大锅，却从两口增加到二十口，从二十口增加到一百口。乔家的粥"插上筷子不倒，解开布包不散"，硬是把"稀粥"做成了"干饭"。

山西财经大学晋商研究院院长　王书华

山西"老醯儿"的抠门儿，全国有名，人称"九毛九"。他们对自己很抠门，但对朋友却很大方。很多晋商的财富，是经过几代人上百年的积累累积起来的，但是面对"丁戊奇荒"，山西商人几个月便捐款近百万两白银。

这些在生意场上精打细算的山西商人，经历了荒漠戈壁的风沙孤寂，战胜了海角天涯的风高浪急，拥有了睥睨天下的巨额财富。此刻，面对乡邻的危难，受"博施于民而能济众"的儒家文化长期熏染的他们，心中的社会责任感，战胜了对财富的占有欲。

山西大学晋商学研究所副所长　刘成虎

晋商深受中华优秀传统文化影响，把"修身、齐家、治国、平天下"作为己任，在发家致富后，晋商没有单纯追求自我物质享受，而是饮水思源，通过扶危济困、兴办教育、发展实业等方式，回馈国家和社会，形成了经世济民、造福社会的晋商精神。

山西省晋商学与区域经济发展协同中心研究员　荣晓峰

晋商一方面通过商业贸易积累了大量财富，另一方面也十分重视对于教育的投入，泽被后世，造福乡梓。榆次常家开办了17所私塾，创下了山西家族办学最多的纪录。其中，包括1904年开办的山西最早的女子学堂，1906年开办的山西最早的私立中学堂，可以说，明清晋商在兴教育人方面，对山西功不可没。

"穷则独善其身，达则兼济天下"，这是中国儒家文化为君子士贤标注的人格高度。在500多年的辉煌商业传奇中，每逢国家危难，每遇民生艰困，不忘兼济天下的山西商人，总是一次又一次地挺身而出，成为历史

山西铭贤学校旧址
Shanxi Mingxian school site

榆次常家庄园石芸轩书院
Yuci Chang family manor stone rue Xuan Academy

祁县昭馀书院旧址
Qixian Zhaoyu Academy site

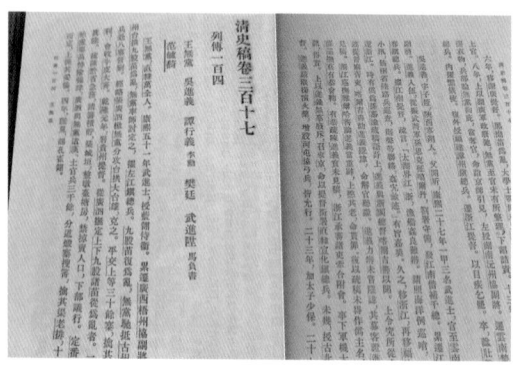

《清史稿》中记载的范家运粮事迹
The deeds of Fan family transporting grain recorded in the Draft of Qing History

聚光灯下那个为国纾难的主角。

公元 1688 年夏天，正是漠北草原水草丰美的时节。准噶尔贵族首领噶尔丹率领三万铁骑入侵喀尔喀蒙古，公然提出了"圣上君南方，我长北方"的分裂要求。大怒之下，康熙皇帝御驾亲征噶尔丹。兵马未动、粮草先行，在长达数年的时间里，庞大的军队不断耗费着大量粮草和军需物品。

为清军承担粮饷运输和军械供应的有许多商家，其中就有山西介休的范家。数年间，范家雇佣大量民夫健勇，奔走戈壁、穿梭沙场，辗转万里、几度遇险。运粮的路途遥远，而且气候恶劣、叛军盗匪出没，运一石米就得耗费 120 两白银，代价极其昂贵。有一年，因叛军偷袭，截走了范家运送的 13 万石军粮，为不耽误战事，范家倾尽家财，凑足 144 万两白银，及时补运军粮，遵守了克期必至的承诺。

据史料记载，康雍乾三朝，范家共运输军粮上百万石。范家的行为，远远超越了普通的商业信誉，他们不计个人得失、报效国家、毁家纾难的做法，是明清晋商"天下兴亡、匹夫有责"家国情怀的真实写照。

中国商业史学会会长　王茹芹
晋商把经世济民贯彻到商业活动之中，在处理商业与国家、商业与社会的关系上独树一帜。早在战国初期，晋商鼻祖猗顿，为了国家富强、造福家乡，便开凿运河，贯通了河东水系和黄河的联系。以商富国、以商为民，成为发展商业的最高境界，也成为商人持续奋进的强大力量。

1

Angus Deaton is a winner of the Nobel Prize for economics and professor at University of Cambridge. He pointed out in his research on wealth and happiness that if every rich person in the world gave one dollar, all poor people would be lifted out of poverty.

This seems easy, but has never been done in thousands of years. Not all rich people are willing to donate one dollar. Even if they all did, how can we make sure the money is distributed reasonably?

The solution to this problem is hidden in a theater built more than 140 years ago.

In 1877 in the Qing Dynasty, a devastating famine whose scale had not been seen in 230 years swept northern China. Shanxi and Henan were the worst-hit places. According to historical records, over 90 prefectures and counties in Shanxi were hit, affecting up to 8 million people. The three-year famine killed almost half the province's population. Trade caravans were no longer sustainable. As a result, Shanxi merchants' tea trade with Russia fell to 4 percent of the normal level. To make things worse, they had to pay massive compensations for breaking agreements.

When a disaster happened, life would be difficult. But something strange happened in the Chang family in Shanxi, a family engaging in the foreign trade industry. Over 10,000 people took part in the construction of a theater, which was not very large. It was hard to support an extended family of 800. So why did the Chang family choose to spend money on building a theater? In fact, they were just trying to help the victims by offering work, as this would protect their dignity. The victims, men and women, old and young, lifted a brick each day in exchange for three meals a day. The disaster lasted for three years. So, the construction lasted for three years, too.

寻踪
晋商

Qiu Taiji, the manager of Rishengchang exchange shop in Pingyao, set up a soup kitchen and helped tens of thousands of victims of the famine. In Qixian County, Qiao Zhiyong forbade his family from making new clothes and eating expensive food. The number of cauldrons he had installed to cook congee for the people went from two to twenty, and then to a hundred. The congee provided by the Qiao family was so thick that chopsticks would stand up in it.

> **WANG SHUHUA, PRESIDENT**
> **INSTITUTE OF SHANXI MERCHANTS STUDIES, SHANXI**
> **UNIVERSITY OF FINANCE AND ECONOMICS**
> The people of Shanxi were known for being thrifty. They lived a frugal life, but they were generous to their friends. The wealth of many Shanxi merchants was accumulated by several generations in more than 100 years. But when the famine happened, Shanxi merchants donated nearly one million taels of silver within a few months.

These shrewd Shanxi merchants had survived the loneliness of the Gobi desert and the rough waves of the sea while accumulating great wealth. Deeply influenced by Confucianism, their sense of social responsibility was greater than their desire for wealth when their fellow townsmen were in dire straits.

> **LIU CHENGHU, DEPUTY DIRECTOR**
> **INSTITUTE OF SHANXI MERCHANTS STUDIES, SHANXI**
> **UNIVERSITY**
> Influenced by the excellent traditional Chinese culture, Shanxi merchants were committed to self-cultivation, state governance and bringing peace to

all under heaven. After becoming rich, they didn't get indulged in material pleasures. Instead, they threw themselves into helping those in difficulty, setting up schools, and developing industries in order to repay the state and the society. Administering the state to relieve the suffering of the people and bringing benefits to the people became principles upheld by Shanxi merchants.

RONG XIAOFENG, RESEARCH FELLOW
SHANXI MERCHANTS STUDIES AND REGIONAL
ECONOMIC COORDINATION AND DEVELOPMENT
CENTER OF SHANXI PROVINCE

On the one hand, Shanxi merchants accumulated great wealth through their business. On the other hand, they valued education and invested a lot in education, which benefited both their descendants and the local people. The Chang family in Yuci set up as many as 17 private schools, making it the family with the largest number of private schools in Shanxi, including the earliest girls' school of Shanxi set up in 1904, and the first private middle school of Shanxi set up in 1906. In the Ming and Qing Dynasties, Shanxi merchants made great contributions to the education in Shanxi.

In difficult times, one focuses on self-cultivation; after achieving success, one brings prosperity to all under heaven. This is the standard that Chinese Confucian culture set for men of noble character. Shanxi merchants had a glorious history of more than 500 years. They always did whatever they could when the country and its people were mired in difficulties.

In the summer of 1688, Galdan Boshugtu Khan, leader of the Dzungar tribes, led

30, 000 horsemen in an invasion of the Khalkha Mongols' territory. He proposed that Emperor Kangxi govern the south and he rule the north.

A furious Emperor Kangxi personally led an army to attack Galdan. Over several years, the huge number of troops consumed large quantities of army provisions.

There were many merchants who transported provisions and armaments for the Qing army. Among them was the Fan family from Jiexiu, Shanxi. In those years, the large number of civilians they hired trudged across the Gobi desert and battlefields, and often encountered danger.

It was a long journey across places with harsh climates and they were harassed by rebel forces and bandits. It cost 120 taels of silver to transport one dan of grain. The cost was extremely high.

One year, rebel forces plundered the 130, 000 dan of army provisions transported by the Fan family. In order not to hinder military operations, the Fan family scraped together 1. 44 million tales of silver, purchased army provisions with the money, and transported them to the Qing army on time.

According to historical records, during the reigns of Emperors Kangxi, Yongzheng and Qianlong, the Fan family transported over 1 million dan of provisions for the Qing army.

The Fan family's acts won them more than just great reputation. They did whatever they could for the state, in spite of personal losses, showing the patriotism of Shanxi merchants in the Ming and Qing Dynasties.

WANG RUQIN, PRESIDENT
SOCIETY OF CHINESE COMMERCE HISTORY
Shanxi merchants put into practice the idea of administering the state to relieve the suffering of the people in their commercial activities. The way they

dealt with the relationship between commerce and state, and commerce and society was unique. In the early Warring States period, Yi Dun, the ancestor of Shanxi Merchants, had a canal dug to connect the Yellow River with the rivers east of it in order to make the state prosperous and to bring benefits to the people in his hometown. Their highest aspiration was to conduct business to make the state richer and to bring benefits to the people. They kept pace with the times. This was the force that drove them forward.

贰

公元 1907 年，20 世纪初一个普通的年份。这一年，美国爆发了 20 世纪首次全球性金融危机；在法国，世界上第一架直升飞机起飞。也是这一年，在山西这片古老的黄土地上，电灯，这一西方工业文明的产物，率先在山西大学堂点亮。因为当时的发电机是用蒸汽传动，所以它发出的电力很微弱，只能供山西大学堂中西两斋照明。但就是这一束微光，不仅从此改变了人们数千年来日落而息的生活习惯，也驱动了清末民初山西民族工业发展的引擎。

就在山西大学堂自己发电照明的第二年，山西商人刘笃敬就匆匆赶赴天津，花 3 万两白银买回一台美国产的发电机。但他此举却不是为了照亮自家的庭院或工厂，而是要创建山西第一座火力发电厂。

山西大学堂旧址
The former site of Shanxi University

山西省电力公司史志办原主任
山西省地方志学会副会长　卢晓山

刘笃敬的家族非常富有，他也是一位接受维新思想、胸怀实业救国理想的商人。后来他到欧美、日本考察，感到只有电力才能推动工业革命，所以他回国以后，决心在太原南肖墙建设山西第一个公用发电公司。

公元 1909 年 10 月，刘笃敬创办的太原电灯公司开始发电，柳巷、桥头街、天地坛等几条商业街被率先点亮，市民们奔走相告，从四面八方赶来，挤进这被电光照亮的夜生活。但在刘笃敬

1908 灯厂
1908 Lamp Factory

钟楼街
Bell Tower Street

看来,眼前熙熙攘攘的人流还远远不够。怎样才能让更多的山西人认识电力,认识他的电灯公司呢?

山西省电力公司史志办原主任
山西省地方志学会副会长　卢晓山

当时太原有个面粉厂,就是用太原电灯公司的电力加工面粉。他(刘笃敬)在面粉的面袋上,印上红、黄、绿电灯牌的电力广告。通过广告宣传电力,弘扬电力这个新生事物。

太原电灯公司很快声名鹊起,各地的晋商纷纷效仿开办电厂。从家用照明到点亮商号作坊;从驱动纺织厂的机器到助力煤矿开采……一股股电流涌动,似乎在一夜之间引爆了山西民族工业积蓄已久的巨大能量。

面粉袋上的电力广告
An advertisement for electricity on a flour bag

> **中国经济史学会会长**
> **中国社会科学院资深研究员　魏明孔**
>
> 1895年以后，西方列强的商品、资金大量涌入中国，使得我国经济受到了很大的冲击。在这种情况下，晋商也意识到应该实业救国、实业兴邦。

公元1914年6月，一名19岁的塞尔维亚青年，在萨拉热窝点燃了第一次世界大战的导火索。欧洲列强陷入混战，无暇东顾，客观上成就了中国民族工业生长的黄金时代。根据美国经济史学者托马斯·罗斯基的数据显示：1912年到1927年之间，中国工业年平均增长率高达15%。此刻的山西，几代晋商用心血铺就的青石板大街，已褪去了"中国金融中心"的昔日繁华。心怀实业救国理想的山西商人，一头扎进中国民族工业崛起的滚滚洪流中。

祁县商人集资3万两白银，开办益晋染织厂；平遥商人筹资9万银元，组建金井火柴公司；山西银行联合榆次富商成立晋华纺织股份公司……到20世纪20年代，晋商故里榆次、太谷、祁县、平遥、介休等地，已逐渐成长起一批规模化的近代工商企业。

公元1915年2月，巴拿马万国博览会在美国盛大开幕，世界精品云集旧金山。博览会"中国日"当天，美国前总统罗斯福来到中国馆，走到汾酒展台前，拿起一瓶酒仔细端详，工作人员赶紧拧开瓶盖让罗斯福尝尝。霎那间，清香四溢、满馆皆香，罗斯福连称"好酒！好酒！"随后工作人员赠予罗斯福一瓶汾酒，据说他一直不舍得喝，直到圣诞节那天，他才郑

益晋染织厂旧址
Yi Jin dyeing and weaving factory site

晋华纺织厂旧址
Jinhua textile factory site

重地打开酒瓶，请全家人一起品尝中国美酒。就是在这届博览会上，老白汾酒获得甲等金质大奖章，而它的创始人是一位 14 岁入行、26 岁已破格擢升大掌柜的传奇商人——杨得龄。

山西省社科院原副院长　高春平

汾酒在巴拿马博览会上一炮打响，声誉鹊起。为了进一步开拓市场，扩大销路，1919 年，杨得龄在太原开办了晋裕汾酒公司，"义泉涌"在汾阳负责生产，晋裕汾酒公司就专门管理销售，形成产运销一条链，全链条地进行现代企业生产制度方法，把汾酒做得更大更强，也使汾酒成为中国近代最大的白酒企业。

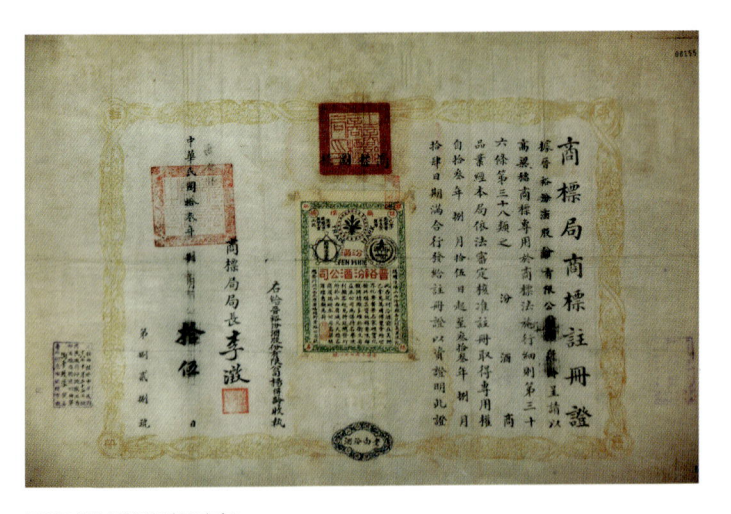

公元 1924 年，晋裕汾酒股份有限公司率先注册了中国白酒行业的第一枚商标——高粱穗汾酒商标，标志着中国白酒产业开始走上品牌化发展道路。从经营传统的食品加工、长途贩运、银号票号到开办

民国时期高粱穗汾酒商标
The trademark of sorghum Sui Fen liquor during the Republic of China

汾酒博物馆
Fenjiu Museum

矿业、炼钢修路、竞逐化工轻纺等千行百业，从前店后厂的作坊式经营到建立科学高效的现代企业制度，从富裕家族、造福乡梓到实业救国、实业兴国的价值延展……

什么样的力量，驱动了20世纪初山西商人的集体觉醒和全面转型？是企业家竞逐产业蓝海的职业天性，更是一代晋商经世济民、心怀天下的精神品格。他们坚信，人生的厚度不在于财富的累积，只有在国家兴盛和民族崛起中，才能彰显出生命的意义。

2

1907 was an ordinary year in the early 20th century. That year, the first global financial crisis broke out in America, the world's first helicopter took off in France, and an electric light bulb, a product of western industrial civilization, was turned on in the Shanxi Grand Academy.

This is the former site of the Shanxi Grand Academy, where the electric bulb first came on in Shanxi. Today it's the site of the high school affiliated to Taiyuan Normal University. The generator was driven by steam at the time, so the power it generated was weak, only enough to illuminate classrooms of the College of Western Studies and the College of Chinese studies. Dim as the light was, it changed people's habit of going to bed at sunset, which had lasted for thousands of years, and drove the development of the national industry in Shanxi at the turn of the 20th century.

The year after Shanxi Grand Academy started generating power for lighting, Liu Dujing, a merchant from Shanxi, rushed to Tianjin and spent 30,000 taels of silver to buy a generator made in America. His aim was to set up the first thermal power station in Shanxi.

Liu Dujing's family was very rich. He was open to new thoughts. He wanted to save the nation through developing industry. During his field trips in Europe, Amecia and Japan, he realized that only electricity could fuel the industrial revolution. So, after returning to China, he determined to set up the first power station of Shanxi in Taiyuan.

In October 1909, Liu Dujing set up the Taiyuan Electric Bulb Company. Commercial streets, including Liuxiang Alley, Qiaotou Street, and Tianditan Street, were the first to be illuminated by electricity. But for Liu Dujing, this was far from enough. He wanted more people in Shanxi to know about electricity and his company.

Lu Xiaoshan,

Former director of the History Office of Shanxi Electric Power Company and vice president of Shanxi Local History Society

At that time, there was a flour mill in Taiyuan. It used the electricity generated by Taiyuan Electric Bulb Company for flour milling. The brand name of the flour was Diandeng, which means 'electric bulb'. Liu Dujing had the trademark, which was in red, yellow, and green, printed on the flour bags. He wanted to advertise electricity, which was something new at the time.

His electric bulb company soon became widely known. Merchants in other parts of Shanxi followed his example and set up power plants. Electricity lit up homes, workshops and stores. It drove the machines in textile mills and helped with coal mining. Overnight, electricity unleashed a tremendous energy built up by Shanxi's national industry.

> **WEI MINGKONG**
> **PRESIDENT OF CHINESE ECONOMIC HISTORY SOCIETY**
> **SENIOR RESEARCH FELLOW AT CHINESE ACADEMY OF SOCIAL SCIENCES**
> Foreign goods and capital started to pour into China in 1895, which exerted a huge impact on our economy. Shanxi merchants realized that they should try to save the nation and to make it thrive through developing industry.

In July 1914, a 19-year-old Serbian man lit the fuse of the First World War in Sarajevo. Mired in warfare, European powers had no time to attend to affairs in Asia.

It became a golden age for the development of China's national industry. Statistics provided by American economic historian Thomas Rawski show that between 1912 and 1927, China's average industrial growth rate was as high as 15 percent.

Today, the roads built with the efforts of generations of Shanxi merchants have lost their former glory. The place is no longer China's financial center. Driven by the dream of saving the nation, the Shanxi merchants threw themselves into developing China's national industry.

Merchants in Qixian County raised 30,000 taels of silver and set up Yijin textile mill. Merchants in Pingyao raised 90,000 silver dollars and set up Jinjing Match Company. Shanxi Bank worked with wealthy merchants in Yuci to set up Jinhua Textile Company. By the 1920s, a batch of large-scale industrial and commercial enterprises had emerged in Yuci, Taigu, Qixian County, Pingyao, Jiexiu and other places in Shanxi.

In February 1915, the Panama-Pacific International Exposition opened in San Francisco in America, bringing together products from all around the world. On "China Day", former U. S. president Franklin Roosevelt came to the China Pavilion. At the booth of Fenjiu, a famous Baijiu brand in China, he picked up a bottle of liquor and observed it carefully. A worker at the booth unscrewed the cap and invited him to taste it. The moment he unscrewed the cap, the entire pavilion was filled with its fragrance. Roosevelt said "Great. "Then the worker gave Roosevelt a bottle as a gift. It's said that he didn't drink it until Christmas Day, when he shared it with his family.

Laobaifen, a high-end product of Fenjiu, was awarded the Grand Medal at the exposition. Its founder was Yang Deling who entered the industry at the age of 14 and became a shop owner at the age of 26.

GAO CHUNPING, FORMER VICE PRESIDENT
SHANXI PROVINCIAL ACADEMY OF SOCIAL SCIENCES

Fenjiu became widely known after the Panama-Pacific International Exposition. To expand the market, Yang Deling set up Jinyu Fenjiu Company Limited in Taiyuan in 1919. Yiquanyong in Fenyang was responsible for production, and Jinyu Fenjiu Company was responsible for sales. So, they formed a complete industrial chain, and adopted the modern enterprise system to make the company bigger and stronger. This also turned the company into the largest Baijiu producer in modern times.

In 1924, Jinyu Fenjiu Company registered the first trademark of China's Baijiu industry, ears of sorghum, showing that China's Baijiu industry had started to build brands.

Shanxi had gone from traditional industries like food processing, transportation, and exchange shops, to mining, steelmaking, road building, chemical industry, and textiles; from workshop-style operations to modern enterprise systems; and from getting rich and bringing benefits to fellow townsmen, to saving the nation through the development of industry.

What drove this awakening among Shanxi merchants in the early 20th century? It was the professional instincts of entrepreneurs, and more importantly, the patriotism of Shanxi merchants. They believed that the meaning of life didn't lie in the accumulation of wealth, but in the prosperity of a state and the rise of a nation.

叁

老北京的早餐,从一屉刚出笼的烧麦开始。在热气腾腾的早上,把生活过得像这烧麦一样饱满新鲜、有滋有味。"都一处"的烧麦有着270多年的古老技艺。几张面皮、一盆馅料,在大厨的手里开出朵朵花来。做烧麦要经过16道工序,压花是其中最核心的技艺。24个褶子一个不能少,代表中国的24个节气。

"都一处"非遗传承人　井听听

"都一处"烧麦的创始人是山西浮山县人王瑞福,王瑞福来北京开了个小酒馆,有一天乾隆微服私访,晚上回来人困马乏,想在外面吃点饭,就发现了咱们店在营业,进来

"都一处"烧麦
"All in one place" Shao Mai

> 以后就跟小二说："给我们来点饭，我们都很饿。"小二就把饭端上来了。乾隆问老板："你们店名叫什么？"王瑞福说："我们店小，没有名字，本人姓王，就叫王记酒铺。"乾隆说："这个时辰不关门，全京都就你一处了吧，就叫'都一处'吧。"

春吃韭菜，夏吃番茄牛肉，秋以蟹黄为食，冬以三鲜馅当令，"都一处"的烧麦里包着四季，也包着天南地北中国人的饮食喜好。当年山西人行商天下、四海为家的性格，沉淀在百年老店的饮食文化中。

无论是与"都一处"隔着一条马路的"六必居"酱园；还是同处北京城的乐仁堂中药、红星二锅头酒厂，甚或远在湖北的"川字牌"砖茶……多少老字号，写下了山西商人白手起家的创业传奇。就连驰名天下的贵州茅台酒，也是当年在贵州经商的山西盐商，用汾酒的配制方法在当地酿造出来的。

晋商纵横捭阖的商贸活动，带动了千行百业兴起，促进了经济文化交流，所到之处，带来人口集聚、产业集聚和资本集聚，甚至影响了明清时期中国城镇化的进程。

中国经济史学会会长
中国社会科学院资深研究员　魏明孔

> 尤其对边远地区，比如内蒙古、青海、甘肃、新疆等其他边远地区，晋商每去一个地方，就在当地形成经济、商贸、文化，甚至教

育中心，这样就带动了当地的城镇建设。所以晋商对于中国，特别是明清时期甚至民国时期的城镇建设，意义非凡。

打开一张清代中后期的中国地图，你会发现有很多地名都是直接用远在山西的某个县命名的。从张家口的日昇昌巷到呼和浩特的定襄巷、宁武巷、宁化巷，以及蒙古科布多的大盛魁街；从萨拉齐厅的宁武窑、寿阳营到宁远厅的盂县窑、代州窑，还有丰镇厅的浑源窑、忻州窑……在这条横贯整个中国北部的商路上，山西商人从一家店起步带动整条街的繁荣；从一条街的兴盛，带动一座城的崛起。

山西省晋商文化研究会会长　二级教授　刘建生

蒙古地区与汉民族商品、物流、人流的频繁交易，既融合了民族关系，又促进了城镇的发展。在漠南蒙古地区，有大量的山西人。比如包头，在乾隆年间仅仅是一个小的村子，蒙语里面叫"西脑包"，也就是有路的地方。就是因为晋商的活动才带来了人流、物流、资金流、信息流的集聚，逐渐形成了城镇。仅以人口而论，包头在光绪年间就发展到7万人口，这是相当可观的。

"先有复盛公，后有包头城""先有曹家号，后有朝阳县""先有晋益老，后有西宁城"……在很多城市，晋商，是其商业兴起的原点，也是经济成熟的地标。

乔家大院
Qiao family compound

  2022年北京冬奥会上的雪上项目，带火了地处"晋冀蒙"三省交界的北方城市——张家口。300多年前，这里曾成就了中国历史上一个著名的经济交流现象——"走东口"。

  明清时期，有一条贯通中俄的张库大道，伴随着商道上大规模的人口迁徙、商品流通和资本流动，文化的种子也一路播撒。自古"商路即戏路"，爱听戏的山西商人把家乡的晋剧带到张家口，让这座河北的城市，成为晋剧的"第二故乡"。

张家口戏曲艺术研究院实验团副团长　谢峰

当时的晋商逢年过节都要唱大戏，比如说迎春戏、祈雨戏、丰收戏、定期的民俗戏，以及庙会戏等。那会儿的张家口也可以叫"维也纳的金色大厅"。为什么这么说呢？因为戏班里面的好角儿、好演员一旦在张家口唱红，就意味着他红遍了整条商路。

文明因交流而多彩，因互鉴而丰富。人类文明多样性是世界的基本特征，也是人类进步的源泉。

乔家大院的最后一次扩建，是由乔家第五代掌门人乔映霞主持的。西洋装饰感的大格玻璃窗、欧式的客厅和卫生间，就连屋檐下的彩绘，也在"麻姑献寿""笏满床"等传统题材中加入了火车、铁路等现代元素。这座青砖灰瓦、高墙峻宇的中国北方传统建筑，敞开大门，拥抱异域文化的精彩，感悟不同文明的真谛。不仅是晋商大院，分布各地的晋商会馆，也

屋檐下的木雕火车、铁路
Carved wooden trains and railways under the eaves

乔家大院西式风格窗户
Qiaojia courtyard Western style window

砖雕中的西洋钟
The western clock in the brick carving

河南社旗
山陕会馆
Shanshan Guild Hall in Sheqi, HenanProvince

山东聊城
山陕会馆
Shanshan Guild Hall in Liaocheng, Shandong Province

晋商会馆：明清时期山西商人在全国各地乃至国外修建的专供商人聚会、议事、宴客、娱乐的场所。清代时，晋商会馆几乎遍布全国各行省、商埠，不仅数量多，而且会馆建筑宏伟。晋商会馆的建立使三晋地域文化与外界地域文化相互交流、融合，把山西商人凝练的"晋商精神"和"忠义诚信"的经营之道传扬了出去，同时也学习吸纳了异地商人的不少宝贵经验，使山西商人的经营谋略和经营智慧更加丰富。

大多采用了中西合璧的建筑和装修风格。在漫漫商路上,经济交流,跨越了山海阻隔;文化交融,打破了精神隔阂;文明互鉴,超越了文明冲突。

著名艺术家　导演　张继钢

东方文化一路上传到了西方,把西方的文明再一路上带回中国。这不就是和山西当年的商人,把茶叶带出去,瓷器带出去,绸缎带出去一样吗?是绸缎吗?是茶叶吗?当然是了。仅仅是吗?不对的,那是文化,那是文明。

美国籍媒体评论员　托马斯·鲍肯二世

商路的开通对促进文化的交流起到了重要作用。文化在不断交流学习的过程中发展,历史上交通和商业的发展必将推动沿线文明的发展,文明的交流互鉴也将带来经济贸易的繁荣。文化交流和经贸活动相互促进,可以帮助人们更好地了解世界的多样性和复杂性。这种了解和认识,有助于促进各国之间的友好合作,实现共同发展和繁荣。

3

Beijing natives like to start the day with some fresh shaomai, or steamed dumplings. Their lives are as interesting and pleasant as these Shaomai.

Duyichu has been making Shaomai for more than 270 years. There are 16 steps involved in making them. The most important of these is the folding of the wrappers. There have to be 24 folds, representing the 24 Chinese solar terms.

> **JING TINGTING**
> **INTANGIBLE CULTURAL HERITAGE**
> **INHERITOR OF DUYICHU**
> The founder of Duyichu was Wang Ruifu from Fushan County, Shanxi. He set up a small restaurant in Beijing. One night, Emperor Qianlong just came back from an inspection in disguise, and he was exhausted. He wanted to have a meal out of the palace. He found our restaurant was still open. He entered the restaurant and said to the waiter, "What do you recommend? We are hungry. " The waiter served the food and the emperor asked, "What is the name of your restaurant?" Wang Ruifu replied, "Our restaurant is small and it doesn't have a name. My family name is Wang, so, you may call it Wang's Restaurant. " The emperor said, "Maybe it's the only restaurant that's still open at this time of day in Beijing. How about calling it Duyichu?" Duyichu means the only place.

In spring, the stuffing is made of Chinese chives. In summer, tomato and beef. In autumn, crab roe, and in winter, shrimp, pork, and sea cucumber. Duyichu's Shaomai caters to diners from all around the country. The pioneering spirit of Shanxi merchants can be seen in the food culture of many century-old restaurants.

Many old brands were built from nothing by Shanxi merchants, including the Liubiju sauce garden across the street from Duyichu,the Lerentang drugstore, Red Star Erguotou in Beijing,and Chuanzi brick tea in Sichuan. Even the world famous Moutai liquor was first brewed by salt merchants from Shanxi who did business in Guizhou using Fenjiu's brewing methods.

The business done by Shanxi merchants led to the rise of many different industries,and promoted economic and cultural exchanges. The ensuing aggregation of population,industries and capital even influenced urbanization in the Ming and Qing Dynasties.

WEI MINGKONG
PRESIDENT OF CHINESE ECONOMIC HISTORY SOCIETY
SENIOR RESEARCH FELLOW AT CHINESE ACADEMY OF
SOCIAL SCIENCES
They had a huge influence on the border regions, including Inner Mongolia, Qinghai,Gansu, and Xinjiang. Wherever they went, it would become an economic, trade, cultural and even education center of the place. This undoubtedly promoted the construction of towns and cities. So, Shanxi merchants made great contributions to the construction of towns and cities in the Ming and Qing Dynasties and the period of the Republic of China.

Open a map of China from the mid and late Qing Dynasty,and you'll find many places named after parts of Shanxi.

These include Rishengchang Alley in Zhangjiakou,Dingxiang Alley,Ningwu Alley, Ninghua Alley in Hohhot,and Dashengkui Street in Kobdo in Mongolia. Also, Ningwuyao and Shouyangying in Lasaqi Subprefecture,Yuxianyao, Daizhouyao in Ningyuan Subprefecture,and Hunyuanyao, Xinzhouyao in Fengzhen Subprefecture. Along this trade route across northern China,Shanxi merchants started with one shop and drove the growth of the entire street. And a thriving street led to the rise of a city.

> **LIU JIANSHENG, PRESIDENT**
> **SHANXI MERCHANTS CULTURE RESEARCH**
> **ASSOCIATION OF SHANXI PROVINCE**
> The frequent communication and exchange of commodities between the Mongols and the Han people strengthened the relationship between the two ethnic groups, and at the same time, boosted the development of towns and cities. In places south of the Gobi desert, there were a lot of people from Shanxi. During the reign of Emperor Qianlong, Baotou was just a small village. Its Mongolian name was Xi'naobao, literally meaning a place accessible through roads. Thanks to the aggregation of population, commodities, capital and information ensuing the activities of Shanxi merchants, towns and cities came into being. During the reign of Emperor Guangxu, Baotou's population increased to 70,000, which was quite a big number.

"First came Fushenggong, then the city of Baotou. ""First came the Cao family store, then Chaoyang County. ""First came Jinyilao,then the city of Xining. "Shanxi merchants were the starting point of many cities' commercial prosperity and were also symbols of economic maturity.

Zhangjiakou is located on the border of Shanxi, Hebei and Inner Mongolia. The

2022 Beijing Winter Olympics made this city famous. Three centuries ago, merchants went beyond the Great Wall to do business via Zhangjiakou, a phenomenon known as Zoudongkou.

In the Ming and Qing Dynasties, there was a Zhangjiakou-Kulun Trade Route between China and Russia. Large-scale migration as well as circulation of commodities and capital spread the seeds of culture along the route.

In ancient times, Shanxi merchants brought Shanxi Opera from their hometown to Zhangjiakou, turning this city in Hebei Province into the second hometown of Shanxi Opera.

> **XIE FENG, DEPUTY DIRECTOR**
> **EXPERIMENTAL TROUPE**
> **ZHANGJIAKOU OPERA ART RESEARCH INSTITUTE**
> At that time, Shanxi merchants watched operas during festivals. For example, the opera of welcoming spring, the opera of praying for rain, the opera of harvest, folk operas performed at a regular basis, and operas played in temple fairs. The Zhangjiakou of the time was similar to today's Musikverein. Why? Once a performer gained fame in Zhangjiakou, he would then become widely known in places along the trade route.

Civilization becomes richer and more colorful because of communication and exchanges. The diversity of human civilization is the basic characteristic of the world. It's also the source of human progress.

Qiao Yingxia, the fifth-generation head of the family, took charge of the last expansion of the Qiao Family Compound. The windows are done in the western style, and the living room and bathroom are done in the European style. Even the paintings under the eaves have modern elements such as trains and railways. This traditional northern China building was open to exotic cultures and different civilizations.

What's more, most of the Shanxi merchants' guild halls around the world also combine Chinese and Western architecture and decoration styles. Economic exchange went beyond mountains and rivers along the trade route. Cultural fusion broke mental barriers and mutual learning between civilizations transcended conflicts.

ZHANG JIGANG
FAMOUS ARTIST AND DIRECTOR
The Eastern culture was spread to the West, and the Western culture was brought back to China then. Isn't it the same as the Shanxi merchants who took tea, porcelain and silk to other countries? Were they silk and tea? Yes, sure. But were they just silk and tea? Absolutely not. It was culture and it was civilization.

PAUKEN II THOMAS WEIR, AMERICAN
COMMENTATOR
The opening of trade routes is playing an important role in promoting cultural exchanges. Culture is developing trough constant exchanges and learning. All the development of transportation and commerce in history will definitely drive the progress of the entire civilization along the route, and the exchanges and mutual learning of civilizations will also bring about great economic and trade prosperity.

The mutual promotion of cultural exchanges and economic and trade activities can help people better understand the diversity and complexity of the world. This kind of understanding and awareness will help promote harmonious cooperation among countries and achieve common development and prosperity.

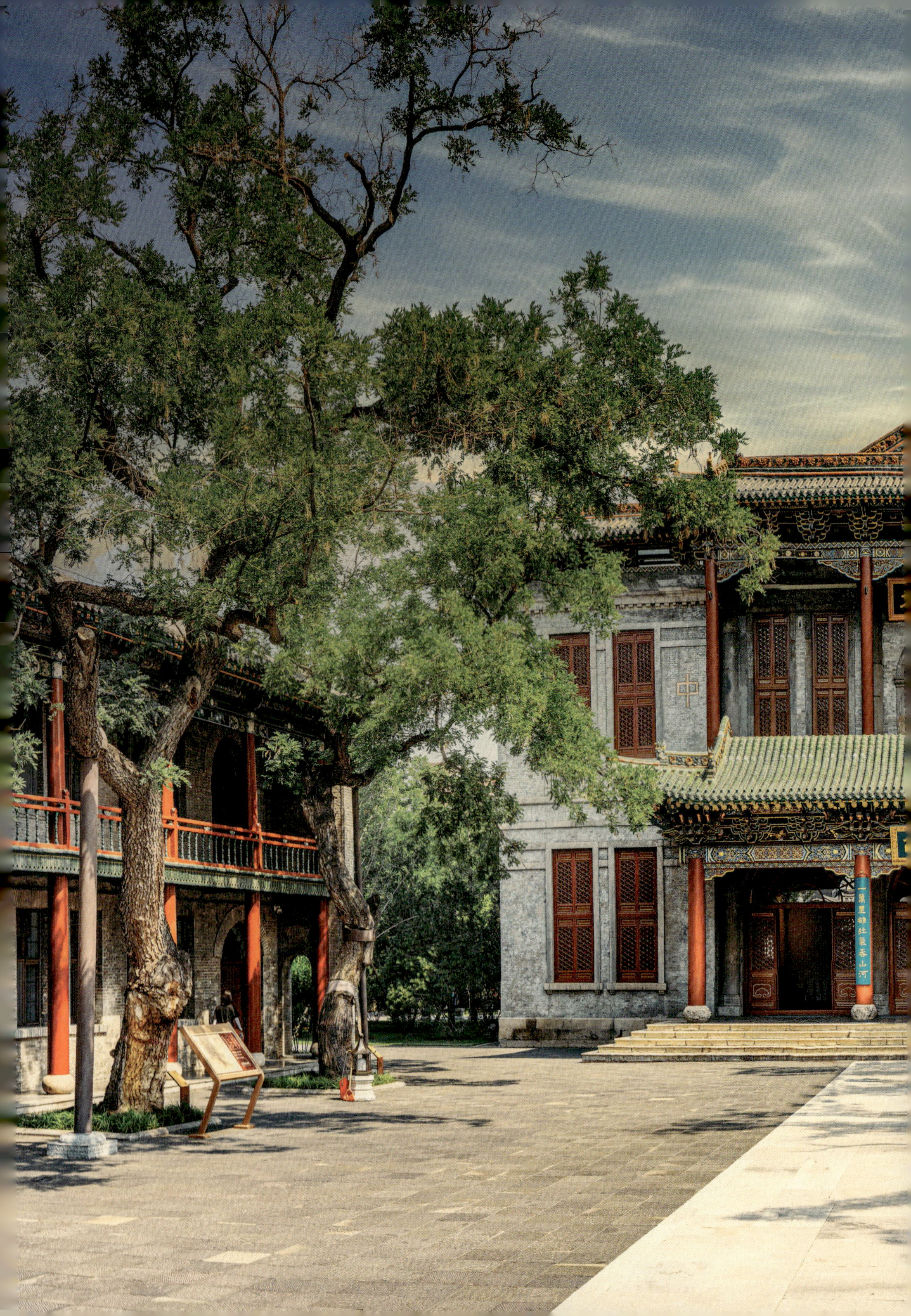

晋商博物院　Jinshang Museum

时序更迭，岁月苍苍。明清晋商的辉煌早已远去，但这个从山西出发走向世界的第一商帮，却在历史的星河中熠熠闪光。

他们纵横欧亚九千里，称雄商界五百年，开创了戍边卫国、商贾天下的商团发展之路，开辟了横跨亚欧大陆的世纪动脉——万里茶道。他们首创票号汇兑业务，形成了金融资本与茶票融合成长的商业路径，走出了一条商业文明演进的中国式道路。

他们的成功，离不开诚实守信的道德支撑、开拓进取的奋斗精神、和衷共济的价值追求、务实经营的商业智慧、经世济民的天下情怀。

承载着中华优秀传统文化精神内核的晋商精神，是中华文明世界观、天下观的鲜活诠释。它蕴藏着解决当代问题的历史智慧，不仅可以为中华民族现代文明提供有益借鉴，而且可以为人类进步与世界大同提供深刻启迪。

纪录片《寻踪晋商》第五集：
《家国天下的晋商风骨》

As time goes on, the glory of Shanxi merchants has faded. This group of people set out from Shanxi, and yielded brilliant results in the shiny river of history.

They crossed Asia and Europe, and played a dominant role in the commercial world for 500 years. They ventured into the military strongholds along the border for trade and thrived. They opened up the Tea Road, a cross-continental artery between China and Europe, initiated the exchange business in China, and developed the commercial mode that combined capital and tea certificates. They created a Chinese-style path for commercial civilization.

Their success came from their honesty, pioneering spirit, their pursuit of harmony, down-to-earth spirit, and patriotism.

The culture and spirit of Shanxi merchants, which inherited the genes of traditional Chinese culture, can shed some light on the problems faced by humanity. It's a helpful reference for the modern civilization of the Chinese nation. It can also provide some inspiration on how to achieve human progress and great harmony.

密押章　Secret seals

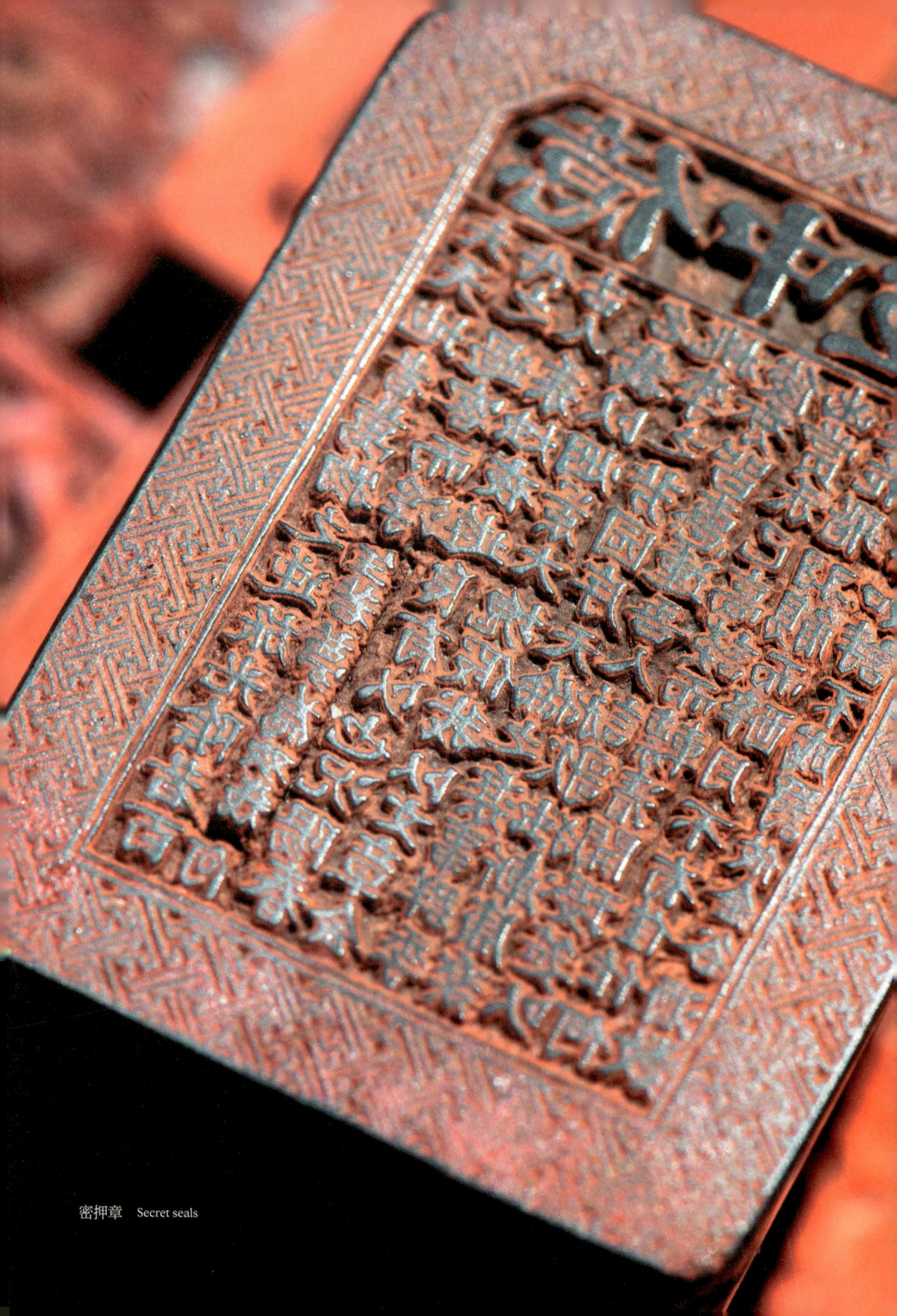

致谢

纪录片《寻踪晋商》通过中央广播电视总台CGTN、凤凰卫视、MC俄语卫星电视、山西卫视等电视频道和新媒体平台以联合国六种官方语言向全球传播，覆盖230多个国家和地区。

在本片拍摄及播出过程中，得到以下单位的大力支持：莫斯科中国文化中心、乌兰巴托中国文化中心、中央广播电视总台CGTN、凤凰卫视、中国广电集团、中国交响乐团、当代中国与世界研究院、中国商业史学会、中国经济史学会、河北省人民政府新闻办公室、内蒙古自治区人民政府新闻办公室、江苏省人民政府新闻办公室、福建省人民政府新闻办公室、河南省人民政府新闻办公室、湖北省人民政府新闻办公室、湖南省人民政府新闻办公室、江西省人民政府新闻办公室、清华大学、北京大学、中央财经大学、中国传媒大学、湖北大学、山西大学、山西财经大学、山西农业大学、山西传媒学院、山西省艺术职业学院、山西省交响乐团、山西博物院、山西省晋剧院、晋商博物院，以及山西省11市人民政府新闻办公室。在付梓之际，一并谨致谢忱。

THANKS

The documentary "Tracing Shanxi Merchants" is used in six official languages of the United Nations, through the China Media Group: CGTN, Phoenix Satellite TV and MC Russian satellite TV channels, Shanxi Satellite TV and other TV channels and new media platforms have spread globally, covering more than 230 countries and regions.

In the process of filming and broadcast, get the support of the following units: Moscow Chinese culture center, Ulan Baatar China culture center, the central radio and television reception desk CGTN, phoenix TV, China radio and television group, China symphony orchestra, institute of contemporary China and the world, China business history society, China economic history society, Hebei Provincial People's Government Information Office, Inner Mongolia Autonomous Region People's Government Information Office, Jiangsu Provincial People's Government Information Office, Fujian Provincial People's Government Information Office, Henan Provincial People's Government Information Office, Hubei Provincial People's Government Information Office, Hunan Provincial People's Government Information Office, Jiangxi Provincial People's Government Information Office, Tsinghua University, Peking University, Central University of Finance and Economics, Communication University of China, Hubei University, Shanxi University of Finance and Economics, Shanxi Agricultural University, Communication University of Shanxi, Shanxi Vocational college of Art, Shanxi Symphony Orchestra, Shanxi Museum, Shanxi Jin Theatre, Shanxi Merchants Museum, and the Information Office of the People's Government of 11 cities in Shanxi Province. Thank you to the above units.

寻踪
晋商